BY E. K. JOHNSTON

STAR WARS
Star Wars: Queen's Shadow
Star Wars: Queen's Peril
Star Wars: Queen's Hope
Star Wars: Ahsoka

Aetherbound

The Afterward

That Inevitable Victorian Thing

Exit, Pursued by a Bear

A Thousand Nights

Spindle

The Story of Owen

Prairie Fire

THE
DRUID'S
CALL

THE
DRUID'S
CALL

E. K. JOHNSTON

1 3 5 7 9 10 8 6 4 2

Del Rey
20 Vauxhall Bridge Road
London SW1V 2SA

Del Rey is part of the Penguin Random House group of companies
whose addresses can be found at global.penguinrandomhouse.com.

Penguin
Random House
UK

First published in the US by Random House Worlds, an imprint of Random House,
a division of Penguin Random House LLC, New York, in 2023
First published in the UK by Del Rey in 2023

www.penguin.co.uk

A CIP catalogue record for this book is available from the British Library.

Hardback ISBN 9781529911398
Trade paperback ISBN 9781529911404

Book design by Alexis Capitini
Additional editorial by Allison Avalon Irons

Printed and bound in Great Britain by Clays Ltd, Elcograf S.p.A.

The authorised representative in the EEA is Penguin Random House Ireland,
Morrison Chambers, 32 Nassau Street, Dublin D02 YH68

www.greenpenguin.co.uk

To Boyce.
This is what that weird girl from Ontario was
working on when she stayed in your house last summer.

THE
ÐRUID'S
ℭALL

In her parents' defense, they did try. They didn't do a very good job, and they definitely gave up the moment things got difficult, but they did try.

And that is how the tiefling Doric survived babyhood.

CHAPTER 1

The sharp twang of a bowstring had a way of attracting attention. Arrows could be quiet if they were fletched properly, and a well-trained ranger could move through a pile of dry leaves without making a noise. But some things were just unavoidable. If you were going to take a shot, you had to be sure your aim was true, because you might not get another chance.

Doric's arrow went wide, and the herd of deer that she and her fellows had been diligently tracking split up in a panic and melted into the trees.

"That was better!" said a chipper voice beside her. Torrieth could always be counted on for encouragement, even when Doric wasn't in the mood for it. It was

the foundation of their relationship and had been since
the first time the slender, dark-haired elf had laid eyes
on her.

Doric crashed through the brush to retrieve her
arrow. She didn't even try to be quiet, and her tail
thrashed at the low-growing shrubs in the underbrush.
She looked up and saw a snowy owl perched above her.
Even the owl looked judgmental. She stuck her tongue
out at it, but it didn't react.

"We can't eat what we don't shoot," Doric pointed
out, returning to her friend's side.

"There are plenty of deer," Torrieth told her. "Maybe
the others will have better luck."

Doric wanted to tell her that it wasn't luck. It was
skill, and it was a skill that she couldn't seem to master
no matter how long she practiced. She knew the other
hunting parties were positioned so that after she screwed
up, they'd be able to take advantage of the panicking
deer. Her incompetence was part of the plan, an exam-
ple of how she was able to contribute. She hated that.

"You know," Torrieth continued, "no one expects
you to be out here. You don't have to hunt with us. You
don't even eat that much."

She did, sometimes, eat what the hunters brought
home. Perhaps if she were a more able hunter, she would
feel differently, but she wasn't, and so she ate things the
elves couldn't when no one was watching and held herself to minimal portions from the communal hearth.
She didn't want to remind the elves that she was different too frequently, but even more than that, she didn't
want to be a burden.

There were deer aplenty. In fact, there were probably too many deer. The farmers and woodcutters along the forest edge killed the wolves that preyed on their livestock, thinning them out until there weren't enough to keep the deer population in check. Then the deer ate everything that was green and below shoulder height, leaving little for the other forest animals. So the elves ate the deer in order to restore the balance. It was a work in progress, but it was progress all the same.

The Neverwinter Wood was a strange place where seasonal norms didn't precisely apply. Something was always flowering or fruiting or mating, and that meant that food was rarely hard to come by. But that food always tasted like guilt to Doric, and if her demon-given stomach could handle fallen tree bark and the occasional piece of limestone, she'd let it. The wood elves had taken care of her ever since she'd first come to the forest, which was a rare blessing from the reclusive forest-dwellers. She was nothing like them, but she owed them a lot. The least she could do was make it easy for them.

"I want to help," Doric said.

"I know," Torrieth said. "Maybe you just need more practice."

It was kind of her—Torrieth was usually kind—but Doric had already decided that this would be her last hunt if she was unsuccessful. She'd try something else. Like berry picking. It had to be hard to screw up berry picking.

"Whatever you're thinking, I reject it utterly," Torrieth said. "And I will kill you if you leave me out here in the forest alone with all the boys."

Doric laughed in spite of herself. Torrieth wasn't the only girl in their age-group with ranger talents, but she'd dragged Doric into training with her anyway. Lately it seemed like a few of the boys were inventing reasons to spend time with Torrieth, and she wasn't particularly interested in most of them. Doric definitely understood wanting to avoid attracting attention.

"Fine, I'll keep practicing," Doric said. "But maybe I should talk to Liavaris about another apprenticeship or something, just in case."

Torrieth only rolled her eyes, and the two girls headed back down the game trail towards the elven encampment. It was a sunny day in the Neverwinter Wood, which was not uncommon, and the air was warm. Outside the forest it was early spring, cold days broken up by warming breezes. Here, under the dappled green light of the trees, the sun wasn't particularly hot, but it could get humid quickly. The elven hunters had gone out at first light to avoid the worst of it.

Now that they weren't focused on the deer, Torrieth's gaze wandered to and fro through the trees. Doric watched her, wondering if she could learn to see the forest the way her friend did. She wanted to love the strong, tall trees and the grappling shrubs that tried to grow up from the forest floor, but she didn't feel it the way Torrieth seemed to. No matter how hard she tried to forget, the forest held dark memories for her, so she could never be entirely comfortable here. She could tell if animals were healthy or if plants were hale, but her experience was hard won. And yet Torrieth breathed the forest in, always knowing exactly where she was and re-membering every leaf and twig she saw.

"Berries." Torrieth pointed away from the game trail. She knew Doric hated to come home empty-handed. "Did you bring a bag?"

Doric had already pulled a foraging bag out of her satchel. The girls went into the brush, and a few steps later, they were surrounded by fat red partridgeberries, dark as blood. It took them only a few minutes to fill the bag, stripping three-quarters of the berries from every plant, leaving some for the birds. They were nearly back to the trail when one of the other hunting parties caught up with them.

"Torrieth, look!" Deverel was almost staggering under the weight of the young deer he carried across his shoulders. He'd been part of their training group, and this was his first successful hunt. He was clearly thrilled. "It was awesome. The deer came crashing through where we were set up, and my shot was perfect."

Doric could see he was telling the truth. There was almost no blood, and from her angle, the deer looked unmarked. Deverel was right to be proud of himself, and he was genuine enough that it wasn't obnoxious. He'd practiced his aim day and night for months now. Torrieth congratulated him, and Deverel's copper skin flushed a few shades pinker.

"Doric, Torrieth," said Deverel's mentor, a seasoned ranger named Fenjor. "I'm glad we found you. I've got to get this one back to camp, but there's something strange going on southwest of here, by the river. It's too quiet, and the water doesn't feel right. We didn't have time to check it out before the deer came. Could you make sure nothing is amiss?"

"Of course," Doric said. She handed over the berries a bit reluctantly. She was going to be empty-handed after all. But there was no way she'd say no to a request from one of the elders.

"Oh, these are perfect," Deverel said, looking into the bag. "Your berries and my deer wrapped up and roasted together all afternoon—it's going to be delicious. I'm going to tell everyone."

Fenjor rolled his eyes, but his smile was indulgent. Torrieth covered her smirk by checking her quiver. Of all the clan members, Deverel was the one she liked best after Doric, though as far as Doric knew, neither of them had talked to the other about it.

"Ready to go?" Torrieth asked.

"Always," Doric replied.

They plunged back into the forest in the direction that Fenjor and Deverel had come from. It was an easy walk through the underbrush. The way down to the river was always easier than the way home. For most of its course through the Neverwinter Wood, the river was slow and meandering, its banks gentle. Near the camp, the river was narrow and quick, with steep, rocky banks that were easy enough to scramble down but a challenge to climb. Doric would never complain. At least she wouldn't have to do it carrying a deer.

"Deverel seems nice," Doric said after a few moments walking in silence.

"Oh, he's absolutely gone on me," Torrieth said. "We could have collected a basket full of slugs, and he'd still be all excited at the idea that we worked together to get dinner. It's kind of cute."

Doric snorted. She'd been with the elves since she was a child, but sometimes the things they did still perplexed her.

"You laugh, but someday someone's going to look at those pretty red curls and fall head over heels for you," Torrieth said.

Most of the wood elves had brown hair, though a few, like Torrieth, had darker shades. Doric's hair color was the least of her concerns when it came to her head. Her horns gave her away as a tiefling instantly, and just as quickly many equated her with the destructive tendencies of demons. Doric had spent almost every waking moment since the elves had taken her in doing her best to make sure that they had no reason to think poorly of her.

"You're making that face again," Torrieth said. "I'm not sure how many times I can reject your thoughts in one day."

Torrieth's complete refusal to be put off by Doric's horns, tail, and general insecurity was one of her best qualities. She'd been adamant about her friendship since the girls had first met, when Doric had spent her first season with the elves. Doric had been mystified as to why Torrieth had taken to her so quickly. Torrieth eventually confessed that at first it had been sheer stubbornness: her uncle had been one of the few who'd wanted

Doric to leave. The more time they had spent together, though, the truer Torrieth's affections had become. In the near decade since, Torrieth had never wavered, even when some of the others expressed distaste for Doric.

They continued down to the river, which was flowing cheerily over the rocky bed. The water was clear and cold, no matter how warm the forest got. It wasn't immediately obvious why Fenjor had said the water didn't feel right, but he was much more experienced than they were.

"Let's go downstream," Doric said. "Upstream must be fine, because the water's still clear."

They kept going, and Doric began to sense that something was wrong. Dark memories of the forest, the unpredictable flooding preceded by too-quiet animals and birds, pulled at the back of her mind. She didn't want to think about it, not even to do what Fenjor had asked.

"Being out here is giving me the creeps," Doric said.

"Do you think we should go back up?" Torrieth asked.

Doric considered it. "No. We'll just take a quick look and then decide what to do from there."

The girls moved as quietly as they could, which for Torrieth was totally silent. Doric felt like a mammoth by comparison, even though none of the animals around them seemed to notice her. They followed the riverbank around several bends, and just when Doric was mentally kicking herself for coming up empty on even a simple scouting run, they came upon what they were looking for.

A huge pile of logs stood on the far side of the river. The branches had been stripped away, and all of the detritus had been swept into a giant pit that was still smoking. All around the pile were tree stumps, short and hacked off, and the brush had been thoroughly trampled. A few of the logs had been stretched across the river. The water flowed over them, but it was clear that when they were ready to transport the timber, there would be a dam.

"What is happening?" Torrieth asked, but Doric knew the signs.

"Humans," she hissed. "These trees are probably worth a lot of money."

"We're still in the middle of the woods," Torrieth pointed out. "Why are they cutting down trees here? How are they going to get all the logs out of the forest?"

Doric remembered the rush of water, the endless drag and pull.

"If they finish the dam, the water will build up behind it," Doric said. "It'll flood the area we're standing on, but when they break the dam apart, all that water will go downstream really fast."

"Pushing the logs all the way to the city," Torrieth finished.

They stared at the wood and water, envisioning the surge and all that it would sweep away.

"I don't like this," Torrieth said. "There have always been humans in the Neverwinter Wood, but not like this. The woodcutters we know wouldn't cause this kind of damage. And it's more than just the trees: this will throw off hunting patterns—and not only ours."

Doric didn't like it when humans did anything, but this in particular dug under her skin. Like with hunting deer, the elves respected that some trees had to be cut. When wood was dead or someone needed a house or to stay warm outside the forest, they felled only the amount they needed. But this was on a devastatingly larger scale. And it seemed like it was just the beginning.

"We should go back," Doric said. "We have to tell the others right away."

"They'll have a better idea of what to do," Torrieth agreed with a wise nod.

From across the cleared area came an angry roar. Doric and Torrieth froze immediately, recognizing the sound. Elves and bears usually avoided one another in the forest, but if Torrieth was right and the logging had disrupted the bear's hunting, it might be hungry enough to try its luck on other territory and prey. Doric grabbed Torrieth's shoulder and they both dropped to the ground.

The bear crashed into view. Thankfully, it was both upwind and on the other side of the river. The bear shambled around the logging stand, sniffing at piles of wood and traces of human habitation. It made its way to the water and splashed its front paws in the shallows.

"There should be fish," Torrieth breathed so quietly in Doric's ear that she almost thought she'd imagined it. "It's probably more interested in food."

While Torrieth deduced the reason for the bear's appetite, Doric could imagine its rage. It should be well fed and happy. This was the Neverwinter Wood; this was a bear's paradise. Yet now its territory had been spoiled. It would have to stay and starve or leave and fight for a new home.

"Very slowly," Torrieth said. "While it's in the water. Follow me."

Torrieth slid through the brush, and Doric followed, choosing every step with utmost care. In spite of her very best attempt to stay quiet, she broke a stick underfoot, and the dry crack might as well have been a thunderclap. Both girls froze, and the bear looked right at them.

"Make yourself big!" said Torrieth, no longer needing to be quiet. "Don't run. Stand your ground!"

She swiftly turned towards the bear and planted her feet shoulder width apart with her arms outstretched. Doric meant to match her friend's movements but caught her foot on a tangle of roots. Her ankle buckled, and Doric went down with it. Down like a prey animal.

"Doric!" Torrieth strained to keep her voice calm. The bear needed only seconds to cross the river, and it stalked up to Doric with its ears laid back. A low growl rumbled in its throat. It snapped its jaws threateningly.

In a panic, Doric stood up to her full height and faced the bear down. It was just over her wingspan's length away, salivating and desperate.

"Stop!" she said, one hand held up imperiously, her legs trembling.

The bear stopped. It stood up and tilted its head, sniffing the air inquisitively. They stared at each other. In that moment, the massive creature seemed to soften, its face all but pleading.

"We're going to help," Doric said firmly. "We can't help if you eat us."

The bear huffed, an almost petulant sound. Its sad eyes were sunken into its head from weight loss. Its fur had become dull and patchy. Doric remembered being so hungry she thought her stomach would chew right through her spine.

"Stay back." Doric set her jaw.

She felt her blood boil—not at the bear, but for it. The bear wouldn't be baring its teeth at them if its home hadn't been ruined. It wasn't wrong to be angry.

The tranquility between tiefling and bear suddenly snapped. Fury once again filled the bear's eyes. It dropped to its front paws with a heavy thud and roared at the top of its lungs.

"Doric, back away." Torrieth's voice tore from a whisper to a cry. "Keep your arms up and back away!"

The bear snapped its attention past Doric and effortlessly bolted towards Torrieth. With a terrifying snarl, it swiped a dense paw at the elf. She was nimble, but not nimble enough to escape the bear's claws. The razor-sharp tips caught her skin and dragged five weeping red lines across her bicep.

"STAY BACK!" Doric shouted from deep in her gut, fingers curled like talons. She stamped the ground and closed the gap to be closer to the starving bear than any self-preservation instinct would normally have allowed.

Suddenly, the bear hushed. It stopped, already in motion for the final blow, and nearly stumbled straight into Torrieth. It ducked its head low, and for a second that seemed entirely like fantasy, it looked afraid. The bear backed up a few steps before turning and running back into the woods from which it came.

"How—" Torrieth panted, clamping her hand down on her wounds. "How did you do that?"

"I . . . don't know," Doric said. She didn't want to talk about it. It was new and different, and Doric had spent a lot of time trying not to be new or different. "Let's get out of here. We need someone to take care of your arm right away." She tore a length of fabric from her sleeve and wrapped it tightly around Torrieth's bicep. She could still feel that famished, angry roar in her ears.

The girls didn't talk as they made their way back home. Doric stared at her feet as they walked, allowing her vision to lose focus. Torrieth was hurt, and all because of her. Long before they reached the treetop village, they smelled roasting meat and heard the clan celebrating Deverel's first hunt. It was familiar, an almost-home. And somehow, she'd have to tell the people who had taken pity on her what they'd seen on the riverbank, what she sensed might be coming, and that she'd gotten her only close friend hurt.

CHAPTER 2

There were enough elves spread across the realms that making generalized comments about their living habits was next to pointless. The clan that had welcomed Doric had lived in and with the Neverwinter Wood for generations and didn't need to move around much to follow seasonal rhythms. High up in the trees, the wood elves built intricate treehouses, platforms connected by sturdy walkways, and broad verandas where many could gather. Dwellings had roofs of woven grass and reeds with waterproof hides beneath to keep out the rain. They didn't have fires inside, though some of the elders had braziers that could be filled with bright embers on nights when there was a chill. There were large huts for extended families, small huts for one or two people who wanted privacy, and everything in between.

Doric's hut was one of the newer ones. Torrieth had helped her build it two years ago when she moved out of Liavaris's home. The elder had kept Doric as close as family but respected the tiefling's wish for a place of her own. Now Liavaris's apprentice, one of her grandnieces, slept in the spot where Doric used to, because the old elf didn't want to be alone.

"Then why don't you move in with us?" Liavaris's youngest niece, Sarasri, had asked. "We have plenty of room."

Liavaris had watched as three elf babies wrestled on the floor, getting under the feet of the adults who were working, while fourteen other children careened in and out of the enclosure.

"I said I didn't want to be alone," the old elf said. "Not that I wanted to be surrounded by complete mayhem. I get enough of that at council meetings."

And so everyone ended up more or less where they wanted to be. The grandniece certainly had no complaints about her new, significantly quieter, living arrangements.

Doric's bungalow was built on a sturdy branch that was usually downwind of the main gathering area. Torrieth had chosen the spot, guessing (correctly) that if Doric were left to her own devices, she'd live in the farthest corner she could wedge herself into. Instead, she was just outside the main circle, with a tiny firepit of her own and a straight line of sight to the central hearth. It was an acceptable compromise for everyone.

The central fire was already roaring when the girls returned to camp. A large portion of Deverel's deer was on a spit, slowly turning above the crackling flames. Deverel had been true to his word: Doric could see the dark red juice of the berries he'd stuffed it with dripping into the fire as they roasted and burst out of their skins. The rest of the deer was being portioned off for drying or smoking, with the hide and bones set aside for later use. The mood was celebratory, and Deverel himself was seated next to the elders while his parents beamed at him from across the fire.

When he saw them, Deverel nearly bounced out of his seat in his enthusiasm to wave them over. Torrieth blushed and pulled her cloak over her arm. Doric would rather cut out her own liver than step on Deverel's moment. Their report could wait until someone asked them about it, as much as it was gnawing at Doric's mind. Torrieth was smiling despite the gashes in her arm. Doric had always found it difficult to stay stoic when Torrieth grinned at her, so by the time they made it to the fire, both of them looked convincingly like they were excited to be there.

"And, as I was telling you"—Deverel was clearly winding up the story of his hunt—"the deer came straight at me. Doric must have spooked it exactly right. I couldn't have done it without her."

Doric felt her smile freeze. The worst part was that Deverel was being completely serious. He actually thought she had missed her shot on purpose, to give him the chance. Torrieth had made her first successful hunt weeks ago, and since then she and Doric had landed enough small game that no one openly derided Doric's participation, but everyone knew she wasn't actually very good. And yet here was Deverel, the star of the hour, going on like she was an integral part of his success.

Fenjor looked at her sympathetically, and the other elders reacted with varying degrees of amusement. Only Liavaris kept a straight face. Doric had never been able to tell what her guardian was thinking, and today was no different. She had a few guesses, though. Most of them revolved around Doric being a constant frustration. She wanted to shrink to nothing, to disappear, but Torrieth had a hold on her arm, and she couldn't leave without making a fuss.

"That's why we hunt in groups," Fenjor said, finally breaking the moment. "We celebrate individuals, but we remember that everyone contributed."

Deverel's smile grew even wider.

The cooks announced that the meat was ready and began slicing portions off the roast. Everyone's plate was filled with portions more generous than usual to celebrate. There were fennel and fiddleheads to go along with it, as well as more berries and toasted wildgrains. The taste was rich and green and only a little bit gamey. The deer must have been in good shape.

Plates were passed around, and Doric took a seat close to the fire. It could get crowded on feast nights, with everyone coming together to eat, and since she wasn't affected by the fire as much as the others, Doric had no problem taking the closest place. Torrieth joined her, her face already turning a bit red from the heat. Tonight, Doric would eat from the main meal. There was plenty to go around, and Torrieth would make a face if she ate only a little bit and then snuck away. It was so easy to be Torrieth's shadow. Everyone liked her, and for some reason, she'd decided she liked Doric. If only Doric's aim with a bow could improve, her life would be all but perfect. She wouldn't be important, but she'd be useful, and the clan would never have any reason to ask her to leave.

Wood elves weren't overly trusting of strangers, and yet for some reason they allowed Doric to stay, though she had never fit all the way in. Their skin was a pretty copper with a greenish cast in the dappled forest light, while Doric was pale as a porcelain dinner plate. No one had her hair color either. But those two things were the least of her differences. A tiefling was one of nature's inexplicable hiccups—a demon child born to otherwise human parents—and Doric counted herself as such. Liavaris had clearly taken her in out of pity. It was Doric's responsibility to earn the right to stay, and that meant winning the approval of the elders.

The clan was overseen by ten of them. The position wasn't necessarily tied to age, though that was part of it. More, it was experience and willingness to put up with one another. Fenjor and Liavaris were the two that Doric was the most comfortable around, but tonight even they were exchanging looks over her head. She was going to practice firing arrows tomorrow until her fingers cramped, she decided. She was going to get a deer.

"Did you two find anything troubling down by the riverbank?" Fenjor asked, shifting closer to Doric and Torrieth. He spoke loudly enough that others close by could hear.

"What's this?" asked Marlion. He might have been Torrieth's uncle, but he didn't share his niece's affection for Doric.

"There was something in the woods, and I asked the girls to look, that's all," Fenjor said. He was sitting with his legs out in front of him, the picture of relaxation, but Doric knew he was on edge: he was digging his fingers into the wood of the seat beneath him. "I had to see Deverel back to camp, so I asked Doric and Torrieth to investigate for me."

"Out with it, then," said Marlion. He was clearly talking to Torrieth.

"Doric talked to a bear!" Torrieth was apparently done holding it in. Her cloak shifted off of her hurt arm while the words erupted out of her.

Every eye snapped to Doric, and she wanted to sink into the ground.

"I didn't *talk* to it exactly," Doric said. "It was more like . . ." But she struggled to find the words to describe her moment of connection with the bear.

"I think it would be best if you started at the beginning," Fenjor said gently.

"It didn't take us very long to follow Fenjor's directions," Torrieth said, wrestling her tone under control. "We found a logging stand. At least a hundred trees had been cut, mostly oak and ash. They were stacked neatly, so someone's clearly coming back for them."

"Humans?" Marlion pressed. When Torrieth nodded, he sat back and glowered. "They'll never clear enough trees to get a wagon in here, and dragging the logs behind a horse would take forever. What are they up to?"

"Doric thinks they're going to use the river," Torrieth said.

Any eye that had left Doric turned back to her, and Doric fought off the urge to flinch. Torrieth squeezed her knee encouragingly.

"I think they're building a dam," Doric said. "It's not done yet, but once it is, they can leave it for a few days to fill with water and then use the flood to push the logs downriver to the city."

"And the bear?" Fenjor asked.

Doric relayed the story as calmly as she could, trying to make everything seem relatively normal given the circumstances. Considerable murmurs rose up from the listeners as Doric spoke, and concerned looks were exchanged. Marlion in particular looked sour and upset.

"So because you managed to frighten off a ravenous bear, you think it is passable that my niece was wounded?" he snapped.

"It's superficial, honestly." Torrieth folded her arms with a frown, and she did her best to swallow a wince as she agitated her injury. "The bear would have done a lot worse if Doric hadn't been able to deter it."

"I'm sorry, Torrieth. I—" Doric started, but her friend only squeezed her hand reassuringly.

"We can talk about Doric and this bear more later,"

Fenjor said, clearly directing his statement to Marlion. "Both made it back safe enough."

"In the meantime, the woods can survive a bit of flooding," Marlion said unhappily. "Fenjor, have your hunters shift their routes over the next few days to avoid any upset to the animals in the area. Make sure to leave game behind. We'll send a few more experienced scouts to keep an eye on the situation, and once the humans are clear, we can go back to normal."

"That's it?" Doric surprised everyone, including herself, by speaking up.

"What else would you suggest?" The question came from Liavaris, so it was kindly asked.

"I—I don't know," Doric stumbled. The bear loomed in her mind, frustrated and furious. She couldn't stop her tail from twitching even though she was sitting down. "I just thought, well, I thought that humans don't usually come this far into the woods, and they never cut down trees here, and maybe we should find out why?"

A few of the elders were nodding and mumbling in agreement, but Marlion held up a hand for silence.

"No," he said. "We will leave them alone and they will leave us alone. It's better for everyone that way. And safer, too. They'll be gone soon enough, and then everything will right itself. A few days training near camp will be good for our younger hunters."

Doric knew she was turning red, but she couldn't do anything about it. She swallowed hard and nodded.

"Of course," she said. "I apologize for interrupting."

The subject changed with blessed quickness, and

Doric shoveled down the rest of her dinner without tasting it. There was music starting up—it was a celebration, after all—but Doric didn't feel like dancing. She watched as Deverel, blushing to the roots of his hair, held out a hand to Torrieth, and the two of them joined the growing number of revelers. With no one to pay attention to her, Doric was finally able to make her escape. She picked up a few embers before she stood, closing her fingers around the bright coals with no fear of burning. She would eat them later.

Her hut was small, but it was hers, and it was welcome. She threw open the door, letting the late-evening sun cast its light into her domain. Inside there was only a bedroll, a small chest, and a place to hang her bow. She unclipped her quiver from her belt and put it away, and then returned to the opening to sit and check her arrows' fletching.

She worked quickly and efficiently, stopping every now and then to watch the dancing. She had joined them in the past, and the elves always took her hands and spun her about in their circles. Torrieth said she was good at it, light on her feet and aware of where her arms and legs were in relation to everyone else. Firelight brought out the gold in her hair and turned her horns to dark twists on her head. Her tail would flash around her, spinning her more. Sometimes, if there were visiting elves from other clans, they would stare, unused to tieflings but well versed in the dark and demonic stories about them. Her clan might not uniformly welcome her, but they did know that tieflings weren't inherently evil, and they didn't care about the old stories anymore.

Doric worked very hard to make sure that it stayed that way, even when her own mind would take time out of its day to make her feel despicable. If no one cared, then no one would spend too much time thinking about whether a tiefling really belonged with the clan.

The sun set behind the trees, casting long, fingerlike shadows that darkened and spread into one another until the fires were the only source of light. Doric watched the silhouettes of the dancers as they whirled, their laughter rising into the night with the sparks from the flames. Liavaris and Fenjor were still sitting close to each other, heads bent so that they could talk quietly. It made Doric nervous. She was sure it was her they were talking about, but she couldn't imagine any good reason why.

Doric looked up at the stars. Most people saw the sky with some regularity, but Doric's childhood had been such that she remembered exactly when she saw stars for the first time. She'd been about six years old, and they had filled her with wonder. They still did, more than ten years later. It was a permanence that was lacking in most parts of her life, and Doric always felt calmer when she could look up.

She was fed and she was housed. She could come and go as she pleased. She was slowly learning how to be a part of the clan, not as a child who needed support and guidance, but as an adult who could pull her own weight. She remembered the time before the stars and shuddered.

What she had here was enough.

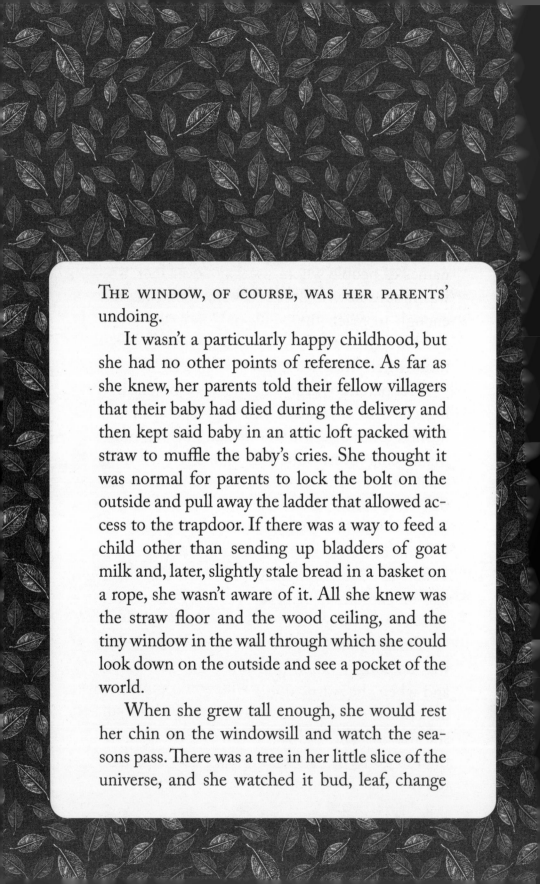

THE WINDOW, OF COURSE, WAS HER PARENTS'
undoing.

It wasn't a particularly happy childhood, but she had no other points of reference. As far as she knew, her parents told their fellow villagers that their baby had died during the delivery and then kept said baby in an attic loft packed with straw to muffle the baby's cries. She thought it was normal for parents to lock the bolt on the outside and pull away the ladder that allowed access to the trapdoor. If there was a way to feed a child other than sending up bladders of goat milk and, later, slightly stale bread in a basket on a rope, she wasn't aware of it. All she knew was the straw floor and the wood ceiling, and the tiny window in the wall through which she could look down on the outside and see a pocket of the world.

When she grew tall enough, she would rest her chin on the windowsill and watch the seasons pass. There was a tree in her little slice of the universe, and she watched it bud, leaf, change color, and die every year. It always came back, which was comforting for reasons she couldn't understand. Her parents made sure she could walk, and she learned to speak by listening to them. She didn't think they knew how well she could hear what they talked about downstairs. It wasn't particularly interesting. The weather, some animals that she had no visual reference for, and names of people whom she had never met. She wasn't sure how long it was before she was tall enough to reach the windowsill, but she knew she'd watched the tree die and resurrect three times when the conversations changed.

Her parents whispered. There was no one living close to them, but still they spoke in the hushed tones of those who feared nothing more than being overheard. Her pointed ears were keen, but not that keen. She didn't know what they were talking about. When her father walked past her window with his scythe or shears, he was in a hurry, steps short and determined. When her mother walked past with her water pail or garden shovel, her belly was distended, and her steps were more of a waddle.

Finally, there came a day when her mother was no longer quiet. She screamed and cried, and when she wasn't doing that, she gasped out directions to the girl's father. The girl could tell she was in pain, and she wanted nothing more than to go to her mother, to hold her hand and tell her that it would be okay, but the bolt was still fastened. After what felt like an eternity, a new cry split the air. It was thinner, more vulnerable, and she finally understood that there was a new baby in the house.

She ran her hands through her hair, finger-combing it as much as she could and picking out bits of hay. She made sure the nubs on her head didn't have any snarls of hair wrapped around them. Sometimes her curls had minds of their own. She split the straw that made up her bed into two piles. She kept most of it for herself, but she put the softest blanket she had over the smaller pile, tucking away the bits that poked out. There hadn't been anyone to take care of her when she first came to the loft, but the new baby would always have someone to watch over it.

The crying had stopped. She could hear her parents laughing. They weren't whispering anymore. Her mother sang a sweet song, soft and low, to the baby in her arms. The girl wished she had the memories of that part of her babyhood. The lonely nights in the attic might be easier to tolerate if she had some recollection of being held. She would hold the baby when her parents sent it up here. She would help it remember.

The hours went by, and the baby never appeared through the trapdoor. She waited patiently, but soon the hours turned to days, and then to weeks. She could hear the baby crying, hear her mother feeding it. She could hear her father speaking in a strange voice that made her mother laugh and the baby coo. And still she was alone.

Eventually, she gave up. She couldn't figure out why her parents kept the new baby down- stairs instead of sending it up to her in the attic. She had been ready. She went back to the win- dowsill. She was tall enough now that she had to hunch over to avoid hitting the roof with her horns, but she could still see clearly into the little bit of the world that was her own.

She lost track of time once the tree grew its leaves that year. It got hot, and she watched the ground bake. It must have been fairly close to the time of year when the tree changed color that it happened, or at least that was what she decided a few years later when she'd finally fig- ured out how human babies worked.

The child that toddled beneath her window that hot, humid day had red curls just like her. The child was unsteady on her feet, but when she fell over, there was no tail clumsily trailing be- hind her. There was no sign of any horns on her head, not even the smallest nubs, which the girl remembered having as long as she'd had memo- ries. When the child shook her head, the girl saw that her ears were round.

The baby didn't look like she did, and their parents let her go outside.

She felt something shift in her chest. It wasn't anger, not quite. It was determination. If her sister got to go outside, then she was going to go outside, too. If it was safe for a baby, it must be safe for her. She had never run anywhere before, but she was pretty sure she could do it. She'd get out there, and maybe find out what grass felt like before it was dried.

The first thing she had to do was figure out how to get out of the attic.

CHAPTER 3

Doric woke early the next morning, well before the sun cleared the trees, and was unsurprised to find the camp was quiet. The clan had still been dancing when she'd fallen asleep, and she didn't imagine they'd stopped anytime soon after. She loved this type of morning, when it was just her and the simple tasks of waking up.

When she was dressed, she went out to the central fire and poked it back to life. She took some logs from the pile, coaxed the flames higher, and set a few kettles of water to boil. She drained the wildgrains that had been left to soften overnight. The fat kernels had split, revealing a swell of white that tasted sweeter than eating them plain and would taste sweeter still with a dollop of honey. She picked up a pail and climbed down to look for the goats, who were left unfenced, since fencing goats was mostly pointless. The goats, who were smart enough to realize that there were things in the woods that would gladly eat them, were happy to stay in the glade and give up their milk every morning.

There were faint stirrings from the family huts already, though the smaller huts were still silent. With the milk obtained and the kettles at a rolling boil, Doric settled in with her mending to wait for everyone else to wake up. She always volunteered to help when one of the others tore a garment. Sometimes, if Doric finished all her self-appointed tasks, she would read a book. The elves did not have very many, but since learning to read, Doric had read all of them, even the ones that didn't make sense to her. Most of them were about the ranger woodcraft she learned from elders like Fenjor, but a few of them were about magic she didn't fully understand. Doric set down her needle and unwrapped some tea, setting it out for the early risers, and then returned to Torrieth's tunic.

"Good morning, Doric," Liavaris said, settling on a low stool beside her.

"Good morning," Doric replied. "Did you sleep well last night, or did they keep you awake too long?"

She got up and fetched Liavaris a cup of steaming water. The elder selected some tea leaves and put them in to steep.

"Bah, they'd talk all night if I let them," Liavaris

said. She swirled the water in her cup, as though that would make it steep faster.

Doric had actually meant the dancers, but if Liavaris wanted to voice her discontent with her fellow council members, Doric wasn't going to stop her.

"I did sleep well, though, sweet girl," Liavaris said. "There was still music when I went to bed, and that always soothes me."

Doric had attempted to learn the pipes for exactly that reason when she was eleven or so, but the results had not been good.

"I wanted to talk to you before everyone else gets up and drags you off for whatever tasks you have today," Liavaris said, skimming the leaves out of her cup and setting them aside.

Doric braced herself. Whatever her guardian and Fenjor had been talking about last night *had* been related to her. And the bear.

"You can't stay here like this forever," Liavaris said. "Stitching up everyone else's trousers and making sure we all eat a complete breakfast."

Doric blinked, refusing to allow anything to show on her face. She could understand dismissal from someone like Marlion, but hearing it from Liavaris hurt.

"I think you can do more," Liavaris continued. "I'm sure of it, actually. The incident yesterday confirms it."

"I've been trying," Doric said. "I'm not that bad when we're at target practice, but for some reason, in the forest everything always goes sideways. I'm sure I'll figure it out soon."

"That's not what I meant, sweet girl," Liavaris said. "You spend hours with the rangers, and that is commendable, but I am starting to think your talents might lie in another direction."

"Oh?" This was something Doric had not considered. She certainly didn't think she was any sort of melee fighter. And, as proved by the pipes, her musical skills were rather lacking. Rangers were always useful to have around, which was why she'd followed Torrieth so easily.

"I don't think you sent that deer to Deverel by accident," Liavaris said. "Or at least not by chance."

Doric had replayed the moment in her mind approximately ten million times, and she had no idea what Liavaris was talking about.

"You missed, but I think you knew exactly how the deer would react to that arrow and that it would head straight for Deverel," Liavaris said. "And I don't think it's the first time you've connected to the animals of our forest either. This is the fastest that any group of new hunters has secured their first successful hunt as far as Fenjor can remember."

"Is that what you were talking about with him?" Doric asked. She flinched. She didn't want it to look like she was being nosy. "I wasn't eavesdropping. I just saw you."

"It's all right," Liavaris said. "And yes, we were comparing notes. I had my guess from a while ago, but he actually saw the hunt. He said the deer changed direction in a way he could never have predicted, bringing it within bowshot for the lad. But you knew. He suspected, and I agree with him, that you intrinsically understood what the deer would do next."

Doric felt vaguely ill. She didn't want to be useful because she could draw animals to their deaths. It seemed unfair. She'd rather do the entire clan's mending if she had the choice.

"And the bear?" she asked.

"The bear confirmed my suspicions, as I said," Liavaris continued. "You do have a keen understanding of animals and an empathy for them that goes beyond what rangers feel. I think, and Fenjor agrees, that you should train as a druid."

Doric gaped at her. A druid? It seemed impossible. The idea that she, a castoff of humans who didn't want her and a ward of elves who took her in, could be a druid was almost unfathomable. Could tieflings even become druids? Druids were all about nature, and humans insisted that tieflings were unnatural.

"How can we tell?" Doric asked, squeezing the words out around the lump in her throat.

"We haven't had a druid here in a while," Liavaris admitted. "The last one was my aunt Sunmuir, and she was a little . . . eccentric."

Coming from Liavaris, that could mean anything from "drank the wrong kind of tea" to "spent the evenings howling at the moon."

"She was an excellent storyteller, though," Liavaris said. "And she talked about her adventures quite a bit. I am sure that if I think about it, I can come up with a way to find out for sure if you share her aptitude."

"With the bear," Doric said, "I couldn't actually stop

it or control it. I might have gotten Torrieth killed. How can I learn to use this? If there hasn't been a druid here in a while, you must really need one, but if I'm not up to the task, I can't be a help to anyone."

Liavaris drained her cup. More elves were spilling out of huts. Even the ones Doric's age were rousing themselves.

"I'll talk with Marlion," Liavaris said. "He might remember some things as well."

Doric made a face, and Liavaris laughed. Marlion was growly at everyone, but Doric felt his bark more acutely than others. Liavaris always tried to deflect for her, but Doric stored up her hurts in places she didn't let anyone see.

Torrieth stumbled out of the hut she shared with her next oldest sister and flopped gracelessly onto the ground beside Doric. She mumbled a "good morning" and gratefully took the cup of tea that Doric had waiting for her.

"You and me," she said after a fortifying gulp, "we're going to murder so many tree stumps today, Doric. They won't know what hit them. Which will be our arrows. I had a healer patch up my arm, so I'm ready to go."

"Did you drink the mead?" Doric asked. She had intended to give the mended tunic back but would hold off if Torrieth was going to spill on it anyway.

"No," Torrieth said. "I just stayed up too late. I'll be fine once I eat breakfast."

Deverel, who quite clearly *had* drunk the mead, crashed down next to them.

"I am never doing that again," he said. "Deer, yes. Dancing, yes. Mead, no."

Liavaris laughed again, showing no sympathy when Deverel winced at the noise. He ground the palm of one hand against his eye and took a cup from Doric with the other. He grimaced after his first swallow but recognized the taste of willowbark and grimly set to downing the rest.

By the time Deverel felt up to breakfast, Torrieth and Doric had finished theirs. Torrieth dragged her off to get their bows and quivers, determined to make the most of the time they'd have to spend in camp. Doric looked to Liavaris for permission, and the old elf nodded.

"We'll talk again in the evening after I've had a chance to bend Marlion's ear," she said. "I'll have more information for you by then."

"What's that about? Is it the bear?" Torrieth asked as she led Doric away from the hearth. "And why does Liavaris need my uncle?"

Doric hesitated. Torrieth liked her the way she was. There was no telling what might change if Doric's new path was fully revealed. Some of the elves were already looking at her sideways as the bear story spread through the camp. The last thing Doric wanted was for Torrieth to ever look at her like that.

"I'll tell you later," she hedged. "It's not really that interesting and it might not even be what Liavaris thinks."

Torrieth accepted the answer with the sort of faith

that made Doric want to tell her immediately, but she didn't. The girls gathered their weapons and went into the woods in the opposite direction of the logging stand they'd found the day before. The clan trained in another clearing that was longer than it was wide. Setting up a camp there would have been awkward, but it was the perfect shape for a firing range.

"Excellent, we're first," Torrieth said. "That is mostly thanks to you, because you made breakfast."

"Thanks," Doric said. When it was just the two of them, she always felt less constricted by the role she expected herself to play.

"Let's get set up," Torrieth said.

The range was somewhat self-sustaining, but they always checked the targets before they started. The stumps they used inevitably became cracked as they were riddled with arrows, and eventually they'd fall apart. It was safer to replace them before that happened, because flying debris was nobody's friend.

"Everything looks good from here," Doric said, running her hands over the last block.

They retreated to the firing line and began to shoot.

It was almost meditative. Select an arrow, draw, aim, release. The sound of the bowstring was clear in the morning air, and even though the arrows were properly fletched, you could still hear them as they cut through the air. The thunk into the target was always satisfying, but it was even more so when Doric hit near where she wanted to.

At the same time, it wasn't enough to make Doric

stop thinking. If the clan hadn't had a druid in a while, then she might be extra useful to them. She just had to gain a better understanding of her connection to the creatures of the forest. No one could object to useful, safe, reliable Doric.

"See, I told you it was just a matter of practice," Torrieth said when they went to collect their arrows. Each of them had managed a spread of five in an area smaller than their hands.

"The stump doesn't move," Doric pointed out. "And it won't run away when it hears me."

"Well, you can't practice on me, so it'll have to do," Torrieth said. "Deverel might let you practice on him this morning, though. I don't think the willowbark will take the edge off his headache for very long."

"I don't think trepanation is the answer," Doric said. She pulled her arrows free and slid them back into the quiver at her belt.

They finished another round before anyone else showed up, and by the time the sun was high overhead, Doric's arms were aching. Torrieth suggested they all go swimming and did not give Doric the option to refuse. They found a pool in the river, stripped out of their unnecessary layers, and plunged in. Doric tried not to think about the flooding that would happen downstream as she lay back to enjoy floating in the clear water. She liked the way her hair spread out around her in the water, and the coolness of the water surrounding her horns. Even though the river was part of her darkest memories, it wasn't all bad. There were good things about it, too. If druids were about the balance of nature, maybe making her peace with the river was how she started.

It was late afternoon when they arrived back at camp, all of them with dripping hair and damp underclothes. Torrieth peeled away from Doric to go to her home to change, but when Doric headed towards her hut, Liavaris caught her eye and waved her over.

"We won't keep you long," Liavaris promised. "But Marlion wanted to talk to you as soon as possible. He's remembered a few things about Aunt Sunmuir."

Doric steeled herself for the worst and followed her guardian over to where the other elder was waiting for them. One way or another, she was going to prove herself.

CHAPTER 4

That night, Doric followed Liavaris into the forest as soon as the sun had set. The woods were dark with the firelight at their backs, but her tiefling eyes could make out the shapes of trees and hummocks easily. She could have moved faster if she had been alone, but Liavaris knew where they were going, and her eyesight wasn't as sharp in the dark. Above the branches, the moon was full, and soft white light filtered down through the leaves. It wasn't as bright as sunlight, of course, but it was enough.

It could have been a pleasant moonlit stroll, but after waiting for the sunset, Doric was too anxious to enjoy it. Liavaris set an easy pace, far slower than the speed with which the rangers moved through the forest. The silvery light made her white hair glow bright against the dark. This was the first time in several years Doric remembered Liavaris straying so far from the encampment. She worried that her guardian might stumble or trip, but the elf moved with all the surety and grace that Torrieth did, just more slowly.

The glade that they were headed towards was one that Doric had never been to. Liavaris admitted that she had never been there either, but Marlion insisted that it was the place. He had been charged with following Sunmuir when she went into the woods to do "important druid business," as he called it, in case she needed protection. He didn't know any of the details, but he knew where the old druid had gone when she needed to focus. Liavaris was convinced that if Doric went to the glade, she'd be able to determine for herself if the druid path was the right one. Doric appreciated her guardian's optimism, but she really didn't think that standing around by herself in the moonlight was going to clear anything up.

It was an hour's walk to the glade, but Doric felt the time stretch out forever. When they finally reached the tree line, Liavaris stopped, gesturing her forward. Doric stood beside the old elf, who reached out and put a hand on her shoulder.

"You can do this, Doric," she said. "Step into the glade and see."

Doric took a deep breath and rolled her shoulders back. She'd traversed glades before. Hundreds of them, actually. Many at night, even. But this one made her feel like she was dragging her feet along the bottom of the river against the current. It was all she could do to take a step forward. She blew out her breath through her nose and walked.

The glade was small, unusually so. It was also, Doric realized, completely round, which was hardly natural. The grass beneath her feet seemed softer—fragrant green as the blades bent under her leather shoes. The smell calmed her, and she walked to the center of the glade without even thinking about it.

An oak tree grew there, bark and leaves turned silver in the moonlight. There were no sprouts around the trunk. No sign that the forest was trying to grow towards it, nor it towards the forest. That wasn't how things worked, but it didn't feel unnatural. It felt like an agreement, though Doric couldn't have explained precisely why. She lifted a hand and laid it gently on the bark.

"Hello." It wasn't a voice, but Doric could hear it nonetheless.

"Hello," she replied, because she was polite, even though she was also confused.

"You don't remember," said the non-voice. Doric could feel it not speaking.

"I'm sorry," she said. "Have . . . we met?"

Suddenly, a shimmering fog began to fill the glade. It obscured all vision beyond the circle of trees and lifted into the air in wispy tendrils. Something like a bird cut through the fog, pitching, climbing, and diving through the air. Its enormous round eyes shone like mirrors. Its feathers looked like they had been delicately carved from opal. When the creature landed on a misty tree branch just above Doric, its shape came into focus: a graceful owl.

"You were smaller," came the answer, "and you were new to the woods. I kept you safe for as long as I could."

For a fraction of a second, Doric had a clear picture of the memory—ghostly wings and silent observation. It was a pleasant one, but it was surrounded by fear and rage and a bewilderment that could have shattered stone, so she pulled her thoughts back from it.

"It was a long time ago," Doric said, as much to herself as to the non-voice that wasn't speaking to her.

"For you, perhaps." She got the distinct impression that it was laughing at her, but not unkindly. "Let me show you again what I showed you before. Now that you are older, maybe you will remember."

It was like a flood, but instead of water sweeping over her, it was an awareness of the woods. Not just the trees, but the moss. Not just the deer, but the beetles. The river and all its little streams and creeks. The elves who camped in clearings and the human woodcutters who made clearings of their own at the forest fringe. She couldn't have forgotten this, not something so big and beautiful. It was like an endless green wave welling up inside her soul, ready to cradle her or to break her upon the rocks.

"That is nature," said the spirit. Doric didn't know if it had a name, but she no longer wondered what it was. "The balance, the scourge. A cycle set into motion long before you were born that will continue long after. It need not be a point of suffering. You can learn to be part of the balance."

"I would like to," Doric said. More than anything, she would like to.

"Then these were left here for you." The spirit drew her gaze to a hollow in the roots of the tree. "Take them with you when you go."

"Go?" Doric asked. "Go where?"

"You will follow the call," the spirit said.

The spirit was withdrawing, and Doric knew it wouldn't answer her anymore. She reached down and pulled out a bundle wrapped in a dark cloak. In the moonlight, it was impossible to tell the color, but Doric knew that it would be green when she saw it in the sun. Her fingers traced over the embroidery of what had to be a crest, but there wasn't enough light to make that out either. Inside the bundle were two daggers, a set of greaves, and a pair of vambraces.

"Doric?" Liavaris's call seemed to come from far away.

"Thank you," said Doric to the tree. As quickly as it had appeared, the silver fog melted away into the midnight air.

She wrapped the bundle securely and went back to her guardian. Liavaris smiled and drew her into a hug. Doric rested her face against her guardian's shoulder for a moment, then she straightened. With a newfound surety, she led the way back to camp.

MARLION WAS WAITING for them, even though it was quite late. A few of the other elders had stayed up, too,

Fenjor amongst them. Doric saw the door on Torrieth's dwelling was cracked open and knew that her friend had probably been sent to bed but was refusing to go to sleep.

"Did it work?" Marlion asked abruptly. Liavaris hadn't even sat down yet.

"Did a nature spirit come? Yes," Liavaris said. "I don't know the other details. It didn't want to talk with me."

All eyes turned to Doric.

"It spoke to me," she said. "It said that it had met me when I was small, when I came to the woods."

"Before we took you in?" Marlion clarified.

"Yes," Doric said. "I don't remember, though. That time is . . . very difficult for me to think about."

A few of the elders smiled encouragingly at her. That child was long grown, but Doric knew they all remembered what she'd been like when she first arrived.

"One of our spirits, from our forest, chose you?" Marlion said.

Doric couldn't stop herself from flinching. Marlion had always been scrupulously fair to her, but she knew he didn't view her as a member of the clan. In his eyes, she was a guest on an extended stay, and nothing more.

"What is in the bundle, Doric?" Liavaris asked, deflecting the unwanted question.

Doric laid the cloak down on the ground in front of her. In the firelight, she could see that it was green after all. She carefully unrolled it and set out the daggers and armor pieces for everyone to see.

"Those are ours," Marlion said. He stood up and

stalked over, picking up a vambrace and waving it around. "This was made by our clan; these are our marks and sigils. We've seen the extent of what you can do with a bow, and you've been practicing that for years. How will switching weapons and putting on armor help you?"

"All we know is that they belonged to my aunt," Liavaris said, her voice uncharacteristically heated. "And that she left them for the next druid who might require them."

She stared Marlion down. With a huff, he returned the vambrace and went back to his seat, grumbling under his breath. Doric felt relieved. She had never wanted for anything after the wood elves took her in, but the idea of having something that was intended specifically for her made her feel warm inside.

"I promise I will use them well," Doric said. "In the service of the clan."

"How?" Marlion pressed. "Is the spirit going to teach you how to be a druid? Good intentions can only carry you so far."

Doric hesitated. She didn't want to tell him that the spirit had told her to go. It would confirm everything he already thought.

"I didn't think so," Marlion said. Her silence had given him the answer he wanted. "What if the next time you talk to a bear, you get angry and make it charge your fellow rangers? Torrieth already got hurt."

"I don't understand how she was able to do anything at all," one of the elders said. "Druids have to study, just like rangers do. She had to learn the basics somewhere."

Even though the elder hadn't been talking to her, Doric knew the answer.

"There's a book," she said as a memory flashed through her mind. One of the older books she'd borrowed to read. The pages had been so delicate she was almost afraid to turn them. She hadn't understood everything the book told her at the time, but she had been compelled to read it.

Fenjor leaned forward, drawing everyone's attention. He didn't speak up at council meetings very often, but when he did, the other elders listened.

"She can go to the Emerald Enclave," he said. "Druids go there for study and fellowship, amongst other things. Barbarians and rangers, too. They have chapters and less organized groups all over the world. That might be a good place for her to train."

Something inside her that was already brittle froze. They would send her away, even though she hadn't told them what the owl spirit said. She couldn't be what they wanted, yet she'd claimed their artifacts, and so they would send her away.

"Sunmuir went to the Enclave somewhere near Waterdeep for a time. Ardeep Forest, I think it was called. That's where she got that cloak," Liavaris said. Doric swallowed down a rush of betrayal. Even her guardian thought she should leave. "It is a long journey, but surely they will remember my aunt and accept Doric. And once Doric is trained, she can come back."

A glimmer of hope caught in her chest. It wasn't a permanent exile. Once her skill set had improved, once she was truly useful, she could return. It wasn't exactly what she'd hoped for, but control was control. She could do this.

"So be it," Marlion said. "I hope you all know what you're doing. Especially you, Doric."

He stomped off to the treehouse where his family slept and disappeared inside. The other elders said their good nights and drifted away, too. Finally, it was just Doric, Liavaris, and Fenjor.

"I think that went well," Liavaris said.

Doric's shoulders slumped as exhaustion caught up with her, and she sat down. She stowed the artifacts away again. She was going to need a bag to hold her gear if she wanted to wear the cloak. She ran a finger down the crest and wondered if she was allowed to wear it. She'd pick it off carefully and carry it in her pack while she wore the cloak. Like the elders' acceptance, she'd have to earn it.

"Do I have to leave tomorrow?" she asked. Besides a bag, she'd need food, and a map, maybe. She could probably pull something together with what she had.

"Of course not," Liavaris said. "We're not going to drive you out. There's packing to do, and we'll pick a few people to take you at least as far as Helm's Hold."

"I would volunteer for that," Fenjor said. "And I imagine by the way Torrieth has been eavesdropping on this entire conversation that she'll want to come along, too."

The door creaked on its hinges. In spite of everything, Doric wanted to laugh.

"Come," said Liavaris, hauling herself up to her feet. "Sleep now, and in the morning we'll start making lists."

It took a week, in the end. Doric's pack was jammed full of gear, some newly made and some given by wood elves who thought she might need it. She had a second set of clothes in addition to the cloak, a sizable packet of travel rations that the older rangers used on long trips, and a large bladder for drinking water. Her bow was newly strung, and Torrieth had given her a dozen new arrows. She carried her daggers in a harness on her back and had tied the armor on her arms and legs. It felt stiff and strange, but she knew she'd get used to it. A bedroll was tied along the bottom of the pack so that she wouldn't hit it against the hilts or the side of her head. Liavaris had given her a small container of the paste she used to clean her horns. They shed keratin even though they had stopped growing, and sometimes they itched enough to drive her to murder.

Lastly, from Fenjor, there was a map. It was rolled carefully in a specially treated hide to keep it from getting wet. Every time she looked at it, Doric felt a thrill run through her. The world was very big. The druids she was looking for were far to the south, all the way across the parchment from the Neverwinter Wood.

Her farewells were brief, since Torrieth was coming with her for a bit of the way. The other rangers shook her hand or clapped her on the shoulder. Deverel gave her a hug and a wink and a pouch of partridgeberries. It was hardest to leave Liavaris, of course. Liavaris had been the one who tamed her when she was wild and consoled her when she wept. Doric could remember her mother's face, but she chose to pretend that it had always been Liavaris. She had been fragile when she lost her mother and feral by the time Liavaris took her in, but Liavaris had soothed her scraped knees and helped her get over her brief discomfort with living in a tree. It was not difficult to wish that she would make Liavaris proud. Her guardian pulled her into a long, warm hug and stroked her hair.

"Hurry back," Liavaris said. "I know Torrieth told you she'd keep an eye on the woodcutters, and I haven't forgotten them either. You aren't abandoning us. You're going away to come back stronger. Even if you can't solve this problem, you'll help with the next one."

"I will. You can count on me. I promise, I'll become the best druid I can be." Doric gently released Liavaris, turned away from the only place that had ever welcomed her, and went out into the woods.

SHE HAD NOT EXPECTED TO *SCRAPE* HER WAY
out of the attic, and to be completely honest, her
parents hadn't expected it either.

The day she finally tried was a warm one. The
tree outside her window had budded, but the
leaves were still a whisper away. It was a little
awkward, lying on her belly and trying to angle
her head just right, but before long she had
scraped away enough of the wood with her horns
that she could pierce it with her tail. She made a
hole big enough to reach her hand through and
then twisted and turned until she slid the bolt
across. The trapdoor opened, and she got her first
experience with the world.

Getting down was awkward when she'd never
had a chance to develop upper-body strength,
but she made it to the floor with only a moderate
bump. The little cabin was empty. Her mother
was working in the small kitchen garden where
most of the family vegetables were grown, and
her father was out in the fields threshing hay.
Her sister was proficient enough at walking

that she could toddle around while their mother worked, so the girl had the house to herself.

She had intended to go straight outside, but when she caught her breath and turned away from the ladder, she was awestruck by the number of things that were lying around the room. Her life was hay and a basket and a tree she couldn't reach, so the idea of things like sewing baskets and butter churns was absolutely fascinating. She snooped around, fiddling with myriad things she didn't know the names of. The softness of the sheepskin in the cradle where her sister slept felt so good against her face. The embroidery and beadwork that decorated the pillows on the low sofa caught her fancy because there were so many colors. The coal next to the fireplace was probably not for eating, but she longed to feel the crunch of it in her mouth, so she took one piece.

Eventually, she made her way outside. Again, she was overcome by sensation. The breeze and the scents it carried. The whisper of grass and creaking of trees. Something was buzzing. Her tree was much taller than she thought it was. And now that she was outside, there were so very many shades of green.

She went over to the garden to see her sister, and that was when the screaming started.

Her memories of the rest of the day were fragmented, shattered by the disillusionment of realizing what her parents truly thought of her.

They argued over what to do. A stronger lock, a sturdier door. She heard the word "tiefling," and even though she didn't fully know what that meant, it was uttered next to "demon," so she knew it wasn't good. When they figured out how she'd gotten out of the attic, they talked about secrets and how they would be shunned if the neighbors found out. She came to realize that *she* was the secret. The unwanted. Her sister had neither horns nor tail. They were hiding her to protect themselves. And they were desperate to keep her hidden. She sat on the carpet by the fireplace and stayed quiet. She was good at quiet. She'd show them.

As the sun set, her mother went into the kitchen and put the kettle on. When it boiled, she poured water into a cup and stirred in some carefully selected tea leaves. Her father put his boots back on, and she wondered where he was going.

"You must be tired," her mother said.

It was the first time she had been directly spoken to, and she felt a part of herself unfurl at the interaction.

"A little bit," she said. "There are so many things to look at."

Her mother set the cup on the table and strained the leaves out. She put her hands on the back of a chair, knuckles turning white for a heartbeat as she gripped it.

"Come and have some tea," she said. "It's

colder down here than in the attic. I don't want you to catch a chill."

She sat at the table. She decided she liked chairs even though her feet swung several inches above the floor. She sipped the tea and found it bitter. She decided she didn't like the taste. But her mother had given it to her, and her mother had never given her anything before, so she kept drinking.

"She doesn't have a coat," her father said.

"Use a blanket," her mother replied.

She wondered if coats were hard to make. She must have been more tired than she thought, because her brain was turning over her thoughts very slowly. By the time she got to the end of what she was thinking, she'd forgotten why she'd been thinking it in the first place.

"Are you sure?" her father said.

"What else can we do?" her mother replied.

Her head was heavy. Her feet swung above the floor, and she leaned forward on her elbows. She could hardly lift the cup to keep drinking. When she tried again, she knocked it over. Tea spread in slow fingers across the surface of the table. She blinked at it slowly, watching how it turned the wood dark and then reflected light.

"It's for the best," her father said with a sigh.

"There is no other way," her mother replied.

Her mother never touched her. Her father wrapped her in the blanket and carried her out of the house. She was facing up, and across the dark sky, she saw hundreds of bright points of light. She tried to ask her father what they were, but her mouth wouldn't make the words that her brain wanted her to say. She fell asleep to his coarse breathing. He held her gingerly, as far from his chest as he could.

When she woke up, the sun was in her eyes. She was surrounded by the trees of a strange forest, and she didn't know which way was home.

CHAPTER 5

Outside of the Neverwinter Wood, it was early spring. The snow was mostly gone, leaving the ground wet and the streams swollen. The tiny white blossoms of snowdrops and the bright petals of crocuses showed in the grass, and some of the fields were green with winter wheat. The meadows were waking up and the earth itself was stirring, making ready for another season of growth and warmth and light.

It made camping absolutely miserable. At least she could wrap her tail around her waist to keep it from getting muddy.

Doric had left the forest a few times since she had come to it as a child, but those trips were usually short, and they were almost always to a single farmhold or a collection of woodcutters' cabins. She knew what a village was and how they operated, but she tended to avoid them for the particular reason that *people* lived there. She didn't like strangers, and they tended not to like her. If she was with Torrieth or one of the other elves, the farmers might only gasp when they saw her, having forgotten that a tiefling lived close by. There was no telling how a whole village of strangers might react, though she had some ideas that made her stomach sour. Doric didn't exactly have a great sample to draw from. At the same time, she knew avoiding towns forever was unsustainable. For starters, the wood elves weren't coming with her all the way to Waterdeep. They would be journeying with her a short way to the village of Helm's Hold, where she could acquire everything she needed for her journey. And then she would be on her own. But the path to the Emerald Enclave was long, and she wasn't going to get any more comfortable with humans if she avoided them at every turn. A few hours after they packed up their campsite, the quaint shapes of thatched roofs and cobblestone streets came into view.

"I'd like to go into town with you this time," Doric said when their party crested a small hill and looked down over Helm's Hold. "If that's all right."

"Of course," Fenjor said. "I think we'll get rooms at the Greedy Goat, in fact. I'd like to dry out the tents if possible."

The hides were threatening to mildew—and so were the girls—so neither Doric nor Torrieth objected.

The jump from complete avoidance to staying at an

inn was rather abrupt, but Doric could hardly change her mind now. She wrapped her cloak around her as the damp evening chill began to set in, pulled up the hood to keep more rainwater from getting to her hair, and followed Fenjor and Torrieth down the hill.

There wasn't much to Helm's Hold. Just a few streets lined with houses, all encircling the Heartward—a marketplace filled with stalls hawking almost everything a traveler could want. Nearby was a small temple to a god Doric didn't recognize, and a building that put out enough smoke for Doric to know it was a smithy. There were only a few inns in town, but Fenjor seemed familiar with them all. They weren't past the trade boundary, as Doric had hoped. The wood elves traded with all sorts of people, so it wasn't too surprising that Fenjor was welcomed with general familiarity. He'd even brought some barter, though not a lot, which was how they could afford to stay at the inn.

Doric hung back as Fenjor requested the rooms be made ready for them. The inn smelled of ale and bread and half-burnt roast, which wasn't the worst possible combination. She could handle this.

"Wrong time of year for you to be traveling, ent it?" said the innkeeper as he counted the coins Fenjor passed him. "We don't mind, obviously, but you're usually here in the autumn."

"One of ours is bound for lands around Waterdeep," Fenjor replied, gesturing behind him to where the girls waited. "I'm seeing her started on her journey."

"That's a fair trip," the innkeeper said. He squinted at them. "If you don't mind me saying, you might want to get a stronger pair of boots. Your forest is much gentler than the roads you'll walk out here."

Doric didn't doubt him for a moment. Her shoes already squelched with mud and hadn't dried out any more than the tents had. Only her footwraps were keeping her feet passably dry, because they were light enough to dry by the campfire in the evening.

"That's a good point," Fenjor agreed amicably. He pocketed one of the room keys the innkeeper slid to him and handed the second one back to Torrieth. "We'll go over our supplies tonight and see what we need. I know the prices here are fair."

The innkeeper nodded and said something about when meals were served. They had missed dinner, but Fenjor assured the innkeeper they had enough food in their packs to last them until the morning. In the taproom, a bard was singing a somewhat bawdy tale about a young lad and a demon, but Doric was already thinking about being in the room and getting warm. It got chilly in the forest, but it wasn't damp like this, and the cold seemed to settle in her bones. She hadn't been inside a human building in years, and she wasn't entirely comfortable with it now. The wooden walls were dark with soot and there was no hay, but Doric couldn't shake the feeling that this place was too much like her old attic prison. She followed Torrieth up the stairs to their room.

"Good night, Fenjor," Torrieth said, just before she shut the door.

"Sleep well," the elder replied.

With the click of the latch, Torrieth threw her pack

down and stretched her arms high above her head. Doric moved more deliberately, electing to set her things down on a chair, but was equally glad to be finished traveling for the day.

"I have had enough of seasons," Torrieth declared. She rummaged through her pack and came up with a leaf-wrapped ration pack.

"I'll have to get used to them," Doric said. "Other places have weird weather, too."

"Well, I don't envy you that," Torrieth said. "But at least it's nearing summer. If the weather were getting colder, I'd be tempted to just tell you goodbye right now and head home."

Doric laughed, because she knew it was a joke, but it didn't sit quite right with her. Outside the forest, she remembered more about her life before the elves had taken her in, and it made her feel brittle. At least the innkeeper hadn't minded that she was different.

"Give me your cloak," Doric said, unwrapping her tail from around her waist. She flexed it a few times. It wasn't comfortable to hold her tail like that, but it was much better than trailing it through the mud. "I'll start hanging things by the fire while you find another ration."

It took several minutes to hang everything up. Fenjor had taken both tents because he wasn't sharing a room, but it still looked like they were living in a laundry. Doric put another log on the fire and held her hands out to the warmth of the flames.

"Here." Torrieth tossed her a packet of food.

Torrieth had her dinner unwrapped on the table, but

Doric ate hers leaf and all. There was no one but Torrieth to see, and she wasn't worried about what her friend thought of her eating habits.

"That's so much neater than my way," Torrieth observed. Her dinner had migrated a bit as the dried foods produced crumbs.

"You tried eating the leaves when we were little," Doric reminded her. "It did not go well for you."

"It went worse for Deverel," Torrieth said with a snicker. "He tried it with tree bark."

Doric laughed at the memory. She hadn't known she could laugh before she came to the Neverwinter Wood. The wood elf children she grew up with had accepted her at Liavaris's command. It might have been grudging at first, and a few of their parents had never entirely warmed up to her, but there were some besides Torrieth who had always tried to make her feel welcome. Occasionally that resulted in an upset stomach or, in Deverel's case, a lacerated tongue, but they kept trying nonetheless. For the first time, Doric felt the full weight of what she was leaving behind. It wasn't just Liavaris and the opportunity to prove she belonged by conventional means, it was all of her age-mates, too.

Being a druid would make her more useful, but it would take her away first, and now she knew she'd feel every league. She was going to control this, and then no one would be afraid of her when they remembered what she was.

"I did warn him," Doric said, a determined smile on her face.

They got ready for bed, a novelty in this case, as there

was a mattress lifted off the ground on a lattice of tightly pulled ropes, and even though the evening noises of a human inn could not have been more different from the noises of the forest, Doric fell asleep.

"I KNOW WE sleep in trees all the time," Torrieth said, looking out the window at the streaming rain, "but I'm very glad we were inside last night."

"It doesn't rain like this in the woods," Doric remarked. It was coming down in sheets. She pulled her tunic on, glad that it was warm and dry from a night by the fire. "At least we were planning to spend the day shopping. That's mostly inside, right?"

"I doubt anyone will set up street stalls in this," Torrieth agreed. Her stomach grumbled. "Let's go see if breakfast is ready."

The taproom was across the corridor from the desk where the innkeeper had met them the night before. Before they got to the door, Doric could hear the buzz of people eating, and she was looking forward to a hot breakfast. As soon as she stepped over the threshold, two things happened. First, Fenjor waved them over to the table he was already sitting at; second, all conversation immediately ceased.

The innkeeper was leaning up against the bar, chatting away with a human in well-worn clothes. He seemed as cheerful and amiable as he had the night before, but as soon as his eyes fell on Doric, he stilled. Doric grabbed Torrieth's hand and dragged her to the table, feeling the weight of everyone's gaze as their eyes followed her. She wanted nothing more than to run away from their stares. The innkeeper surprised her the most, though. He'd been perfectly comfortable last night, and even kind. She sat on her hands to avoid running them through her hair.

Her cloak. Last night, her tail had been wrapped around her waist under her cloak, and her head had been under her hood. She hadn't meant to conceal who she was; the only thing on her mind then was keeping warm. The realization made her even more uncomfortable, and her hands froze on their way to pull up her hood again. Surely, they wouldn't attack her. She had proved last night that she was just as capable of living peacefully as they were. It had just been so damn cold, and she was angry that that was what had made her appear safe. The innkeeper had thought she was a wood elf. And now he knew—now they all knew—that she was a tiefling.

"Doric?" Fenjor asked quietly. There was pity on his face, and that only made her feel worse. Beside her, she felt Torrieth realize what was happening and start to boil with rage.

"I'm fine," she said, her voice a little bit louder than she needed it to be. "I was just looking forward to breakfast. You mentioned that the oat porridge here is good."

He hadn't, but it was the most normal food she could think of off the top of her head.

"I'll get it," Torrieth said, seething, ready to fight as always.

"No," Doric said. "I mean, I'll come with you. There might be fruit."

Several people left the food line immediately. A few even left the taproom. Fenjor was going to lose trade contacts after all. Doric almost quailed. No: if she hid now, she'd never stop hiding, and she was going to have to spend goodness knew how long away from her friends with humans all around her. Humans who disliked her on sight for being unnatural, not trusting how she came to be or that she was capable of anything good. The wood elves—following Liavaris's lead after the woman had taken in a child simply because that child needed a home—had never asked for proof, even the ones who didn't entirely trust her. Maybe that was why she had no problem giving it to them.

Doric stood and squared her shoulders. She walked back across the taproom floor without looking around. She knew Torrieth was behind her, and that helped. The food was laid out so that you might choose what you wanted. Doric took a bowl and filled it with porridge, and then sprinkled honey, bacon, and a great deal of pepper on top. After a moment, she added three berries, just for decoration, and got a spoon.

Conversation returned to the taproom as she sat down to eat, but it was muffled. They were determined that she not overhear them, as if she cared about what they were saying. Which she did, of course, but she wasn't going to let on. The room was tense, but there was no thrum of danger beneath the breakfast chatter. They would be much happier when she left, but they wouldn't go as far as torches and pitchforks.

"Have you made a list of what we need today?" she asked Fenjor.

"I have." He spoke with a heartfelt tone and a shine in his eye. He looked so proud of her that she almost cried. "We can head out as soon as you're done eating, if you like."

She could have shoveled the porridge down. She didn't really need to chew it, and even the toppings she'd picked were easy to eat. But that would have been giving in, too, and she knew that once she started changing her behavior, the humans would win. She would do anything to make sure the humans didn't win.

She still ate her breakfast more quickly than she needed to.

CHAPTER 6

Shopping in the Heartward had mixed results. Fenjor was respected enough that no one actually turned them away, but Doric was definitely the center of attention in ways she didn't enjoy. It was unavoidable, since she was the one they were doing the bulk of the shopping for, but it was still uncomfortable for all parties involved.

The cobbler was the least problematic of everyone they visited, and by some mercy, she was also their first stop. She raised her eyebrows when she realized that Doric had horns and a tail but didn't say anything or even flinch as she measured Doric's feet and calves.

"I spend a lot of time with hides," she said by way of

explanation. "You don't smell worse than them, and frankly, that's all I need in a person. That's why I avoid the tavern."

She laughed, and Doric joined in a beat late, not entirely sure she was invited.

Helm's Hold saw enough adventurers that a few of the boots were ready-made, and one pair would suit Doric just fine. They were significantly taller than her old shoes, and both the sole and the sides were sturdier. Cleverly, they laced up at the back, which meant they could fit a wider variety of people than if they were made to fit.

"My mum taught me that," the cobbler said when Doric commented on the practicality of it. "We get a lot of people passing through. There's only so many sizes a foot can be, and the laces make it so that they fit well."

Torrieth also looked at a pair, though the ones she selected were lighter. She had brought along a few of her best hides to use as trade, and the cobbler happily accepted them. Doric paid for her boots in coin that Liavaris had given her, and by the time they left the shop, she was feeling a bit better about the whole dealing-with-humans thing.

That feeling lasted about thirty seconds. When they entered the next shop, a dry goods store, to meet Fenjor, the proprietor was glowering at them before the door swung shut.

"We'll be needing long-travel rations," Fenjor said, as though nothing were out of the ordinary. "We're not picky as to taste."

The foodseller narrowed his eyes at Doric and then turned to the shelves, selecting things seemingly at random. Some of them were not exactly fresh anymore, but Doric didn't see any mold and decided that they would suit her.

"Will you or the young miss be needing anything?" the foodseller asked, speaking only to Fenjor.

"No, we're headed back into the woods soon," Fenjor said. "And if this is the best you've got, then I think we're better off anyway."

The foodseller reluctantly added a few nicer ration packets to the pile. These ones were the right color and everything. Fenjor bargained hard and secured a price well under what even the nearly spoiled food was worth. Doric paid, forcing the man to take the coins out of her hand, which he did as gingerly as possible.

"He would have thrown it out if you hadn't bought it," Fenjor said once they were back in the street. "I don't feel bad about lowballing his prices."

Torrieth was quiet for a moment.

"Will they always take advantage?" she asked. "Of Doric, I mean. They seem to like you well enough."

"Most people don't like tieflings," Doric reminded her. "I make them think about the things that go bump in the night. At home, everyone's sort of nice because Liavaris made them. And then everyone got used to me. Out here, all they'll see are my horns and tail, every time."

"I hate that." Torrieth ground her teeth. "I hate that people do that to you."

"I'll get used to it," Doric lied. "And it's not so bad. I'd probably like it less if everyone was all cheerful and in my face all the time."

"A whole world full of Deverels," Fenjor said, his voice slightly aghast at the idea. "It chills the blood."

"This sodding rain chills the blood," Torrieth grumbled. "Are we almost done?"

"One more stop," Fenjor said.

He led the way to a store with a pair of swords hanging above the door. Inside was a wide collection of weapons of all styles. It was too much of a mishmash to be properly called an armory, but Doric was still surprised to see so many options. Her eyes grew wide at the display of arms in every shape and size, and she wandered, mesmerized, over to where the staffs leaned against the wall.

"I think that might be a bit much to start with," Fenjor said. "Plus, you've put in all that work with the bow and arrow already. Your aim is too good to waste on hitting people with sticks."

"What do you think, then?" Doric asked.

"Why don't you just take the bow?" Torrieth added.

"I think her best bet, at least for now, traveling alone, is to rely on stealth," Fenjor said. "The bow is fine, but you can't really hide it. If she looks harmless, people will get close, and then she can get them."

"Hmm . . . How about this?" Doric asked. She held up a small sling.

It didn't look like much, but it fit the size of her hands perfectly. When she held it, Doric felt like it was meant to be hers, just as she had felt with the old druid's armor.

"I think that's a good idea," Fenjor told her.

"It even clips onto my sleeve," Doric said, locking the sling into place and pulling it a few times to test it. "I bet it will be even better on my vambrace."

"Are you sure?" Torrieth said. "She's going to need to hunt with that."

"You can get a lot of power out of a good sling." The weapons seller stepped in. If they cared about Doric's origins, they didn't show it. "You put a decent stone in there and hit your target, it'll take down pretty much anything."

Torrieth didn't completely believe them, but Doric was content with her decision. It was definitely going to be easier to carry than her bow and quiver, even if she had to bring along a pouch full of stones.

"All right," she said. "I'll take it."

TORRIETH PUTTERED AROUND the room, gathering up their dried-out tents and dividing the things Doric would take with her from those Torrieth would take back to the forest. She folded and refolded the canvas of Doric's tent, determined to get it as compact as possible, even though Doric was only going to shake it out the first time she made camp. Then the wood elf turned to double-checking their packs. On her eighth or tenth pass, Doric finally couldn't take it anymore.

"I think everything is accounted for," she said. "You can stop fiddling with it."

"I just wanted to be sure," Torrieth said.

Doric softened immediately. She had always done her best to forget those early days, but clearly they stuck with Torrieth. Doric had been disheveled and too scrawny when they met. And before that, she had been half-drowned.

"I do appreciate it," she said. "And I understand why you're worried. I'm worried about you, too. Deverel will have to be your partner for the hunt now, and you'll never be rid of him."

Torrieth giggled.

"I don't think that's necessarily a bad thing," she said. Then she ran her fingers along the seam of Doric's pack again. "I didn't realize how different things would be out here, Doric. You pretend that the things people say about you don't bother you, but they must, ever since the beginning."

"I've had you ever since then," Doric pointed out. "And Liavaris, and all the others. Even Marlion, and he didn't like me all that much."

Torrieth laughed again. She left the pack behind and came to sit on the bed. She was solemn.

"And now you'll be alone again," Torrieth said.

Doric took her hand and squeezed it.

"Maybe," Doric postulated. "At least until I find the Enclave. There's a big difference between being dropped in the forest as a child by your parents and being sent off to learn magic."

"That's a good point," Torrieth admitted. She

squeezed back. "And you have a home to come back to now, too."

"I do," said Doric.

It was still something that surprised her. She didn't know exactly what would happen as she studied with the other druids in the wild, but it would give her purpose, and that would make her a better member of her community when she got back. It was everything she wanted.

Torrieth yawned. "I know all we did was walk around in human buildings today, but I am exhausted. Do you mind if I go to bed?"

"No," Doric said. "I'm going to stay awake for a bit, but I can be quiet."

Torrieth stripped down to her chemise and crawled under the covers while Doric moved to sit over by the fire. She sat there listening to the sound of her friend breathing until it evened out. When Torrieth was asleep, she tiptoed across the room to pull the druid bundle out of her pack.

She spread the contents on the rug in front of the fire. She hadn't put the armor on since that day in the forest, but she was going to wear it tomorrow. There was even a spot for her to clip her new sling into place. She had been planning to carry it in a pocket on her belt, but her arm would be better. She'd be able to practice while she walked.

A sudden burst of rain struck the window, making her jump. There wasn't really a need to detect the seasons in the Neverwinter Wood. Out in the rest of the world, she had quickly learned, the weather shifted quickly, especially at this time of year. It had made her very uncomfortable for the first few days of travel, but she was learning to live with the differences. And the damp.

Now that she was thinking about it intentionally, there really was nothing similar between the walls of the inn and the walls of her parents' attic. They were just wood, and that was the full extent of what they had in common. Doric wasn't afraid here, and she didn't feel like she was straying close to memories she would rather steer clear of.

It was still raining outside. After a few days of walking outside the woods, she was better at spotting the signs of a coming storm. The leaves all turned over, and there was a taste to the air. Storms here tended to dump ferociously in their first moments and then peter down to a gentle mist. You still got wet in the mist, but at least it was easier to make out your surroundings.

Even the human village was starting to make sense. They pushed back against nature because it was the only way they could make a living. Their plowing and cutting were innately destructive, but it was also just a different kind of land management than what the wood elves did. It was certainly less destructive than what the humans in the Neverwinter Wood were doing. Even so, it was destruction, and Doric wasn't sure if the ends justified the means.

Doric wondered whether she should be angry. Maybe the other druids would tell her. For now, it was more a feeling of inevitability. People would build, nature would fight—balance was hard to achieve. Even though she knew it was possible, she didn't see how the humans of this town were going to achieve it, and this village wasn't even very large.

For the first time, she was truly glad that she was heading to the Emerald Enclave. She had questions, and she wanted answers. She would ask them of people who hadn't raised her, who weren't responsible for her. People she could just leave behind when she had studied enough. It didn't matter if they didn't like her, because eventually she was going to leave them. It was a freedom she wasn't used to, and she planned to enjoy it.

She picked the scissors out of Torrieth's fletching bag and began to trim her hair. The mirror in the room was brassy and the light was low, but Doric knew that when the morning came, there would be absolutely no mistaking her horns.

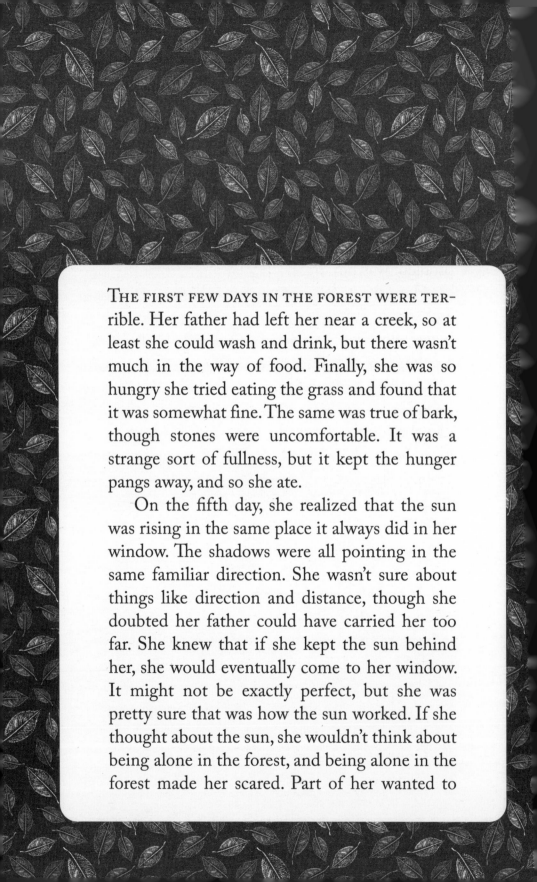

THE FIRST FEW DAYS IN THE FOREST WERE TER-
rible. Her father had left her near a creek, so at
least she could wash and drink, but there wasn't
much in the way of food. Finally, she was so
hungry she tried eating the grass and found that
it was somewhat fine. The same was true of bark,
though stones were uncomfortable. It was a
strange sort of fullness, but it kept the hunger
pangs away, and so she ate.

On the fifth day, she realized that the sun
was rising in the same place it always did in her
window. The shadows were all pointing in the
same familiar direction. She wasn't sure about
things like direction and distance, though she
doubted her father could have carried her too
far. She knew that if she kept the sun behind
her, she would eventually come to her window.
It might not be exactly perfect, but she was
pretty sure that was how the sun worked. If she
thought about the sun, she wouldn't think about
being alone in the forest, and being alone in the
forest made her scared. Part of her wanted to

scream and run, to find a place to hide from the dangers of the wilderness, but if she did that, she might get more lost, and then she wouldn't be able to go home.

She started walking, chewing on tree bark as she went. It quickly got hot, and she had nothing to protect her head from the sun. Once she left the trees, it got even brighter. But the biggest problem was her dress.

Her parents had always clothed her in a general sort of way. When she got bigger, she had bigger clothing. The current dress was a smidge too long, as they expected her to grow into it. She walked carefully so as not to trip over the hem. Her tail was trapped underneath her skirt, and the longer she walked, the more it hurt to keep her tail confined. She tried wiggling it around, but that only made it worse.

Looking around to be sure she was alone, and then feeling ridiculous for doing so since she had been *abandoned in the forest,* she pulled up the dress as high as she could and picked up her tail. It had always been part of her, so she hadn't given it much thought except to avoid sitting on it, because that hurt the most. It was fairly unremarkable for a tail, she thought. Brown and scaly, and long as her legs, with a slightly forked end. She ran her finger along the edge and found that it was sharp. That gave her an idea.

Contorting herself to reach, she pulled at the waist on the back of her dress. Once she had a firm grip on it, she sawed the fabric with the end of her tail. It took a while, but eventually she made a slit, and then she tore it wider. She threaded her tail through it and readjusted her clothing so that everything was back in place. It wasn't perfect, but now her tail was free, and the awkward rubbing when she walked was gone.

Feeling very proud of herself, she kept going. As the sun got higher, it was difficult to tell which direction she was supposed to be going. She squinted up, trying not to look directly at the sun but needing to know where it was. When she was concentrating on things like the sun and the wind, it was easier for her to figure out which direction to go. She walked on, feeling her way forward in a way she couldn't explain, but with a certainty that she was headed the right way.

The sun beat down. She was thirsty, even after she stopped at a creek, and the bark was starting to aggravate her tongue. Her horns itched, and her tail dragged behind her in the dirt. Holding it up took a lot of work from muscles she wasn't used to using, so eventually she settled for carrying it, even though that felt ridiculous. Her shoes were thin enough that she felt every bump, root, and rock underneath them.

Finally, as the sun was starting to disappear below the horizon, she came to the familiar yard that she had spent all those years looking at out her window. She was home. She stopped before she entered the clearing, a new problem on her mind.

The walk had required so much of her concentration that she hadn't really thought the rest of her plan through. She had only wanted to go home, and so she went. Now that she was here, she was faced with the inescapable truth that her parents had drugged her and deposited her a full day's walk away in the forest while she was asleep. They didn't want her. Worse, they had actively gotten rid of her.

She couldn't make herself take another step forward. If she did, she might see them. She might see how happy they were, her parents and her sister, sitting around the table as a family, without any fear of what lived upstairs. She might see her mother dance as her father whistled, something they had never done, to her knowledge, because she took the song right out of them. She might see her sister climbing up and down the ladder to the loft, a game, while her parents watched and complimented her on how strong she was and how sure on her feet.

She didn't want to see it. Didn't want to hear it. Didn't want to know if it was true. They were better off without her, even though she had no idea how to manage without them. They had made their feelings clear.

She turned so that the sun was behind her. She couldn't walk all night, but she could start walking now. She didn't know where she was going. Back to the forest, her heart said, but her heart was broken, and she wasn't sure if it was a reliable source.

Behind her, the family sat down to dinner, happy at last.

CHAPTER 7

Fenjor and Torrieth turned back two days later, on the bank of a small river that rushed white-capped and rolling to the south. They had brought Doric as far as they could, and she had to travel the rest of the way on her own. Before they left the Neverwinter Wood, she had been slightly terrified at the idea, but after just shy of a tenday out in the world at large, Doric felt like she could handle it. The humans were weird, and it was going to take her a while to get used to the randomness of spring weather, but every day was easier, and every day her connection to the land around her grew.

"Don't you dare stay away," Torrieth said, tears

streaming down her face as she clung to Doric's shoulders. "You are going to come back."

"I am going to come back," Doric said. "Where else would I ever want to go?"

Fenjor didn't say anything, which made Doric wonder what he knew that she didn't. He was headed back to the forest, after all. She would be no different. She just had a longer walk.

"Don't go too far into strange forests unless you know the druids are there," he said when Torrieth finally detached herself. "You'd probably be fine, but there's no reason to take unnecessary risks."

"I won't," Doric said.

"Keep heading south. With your abilities, it will be safer if you travel through the woods, parallel to the High Road, where you'll find new settlements," Fenjor continued. "Be careful, but they should be able to tell you if there are any druids around, or if there's any Emerald Enclave activity in the area."

"Thank you," Doric said. "For everything you've taught me, and for bringing me as far as you could."

The elder nodded and then pulled Torrieth's shoulder to get her to start walking. Doric couldn't bring herself to turn around and walk away from their last shared campsite quite yet. Torrieth kept turning around to wave, and Doric always waved back. Finally, they went over a rise and down into a little dell, and Doric turned south.

It was an easy walk along the river, but Doric's heart was strangely heavy. The last of her connection to the wood elves was gone. What if they returned and decided they didn't really need her to come back? Someday she might come back to them only to find she didn't have a place. She knew that Liavaris and Torrieth would welcome her, but if it wasn't her home anymore, she wouldn't be able to stay. Doric knew that these thoughts were foolish, but she couldn't help them. She hadn't been alone in a long time. She forced herself to stop thinking morose thoughts and concentrate on her surroundings.

There was tall grass and the occasional boggy area where the river had overflowed its banks in the spring flood. Most of the meltwater had receded now, but the ground held the moisture like a sponge. Doric stuck to rocky areas to keep her boots dry. Birds flew overhead every now and then, their screams echoing across the empty plain. Doric could imagine the air currents that helped them glide, and the fierce desire to dive with talons spread. Once she started looking around herself instead of within, it was one of her better mornings, to be totally honest. The rain had finally stopped, and she was feeling lighter, even though she was alone.

That night she camped in the lee of the only real hill for miles around. There was a little stream and some fiddleheads for her to add to her dinner. There were also quite a few mushrooms she didn't recognize. She knew that she could eat pretty much anything, but she also knew that mushrooms tended to make their own rules, so she left them alone. She had plenty of food in her pack, in any case, so there was no need for experimentation.

The days went on, much the same. The land didn't

change too much as she followed the river, but the weather was definitely improving as summer grew closer and she traveled ever southward. Doric witnessed the shift of seasons in the grass beneath her feet and in the lives of animals that she shared the wilderness with. She avoided settlements, even when the food Fenjor had given her ran out. There was plenty to forage, and her sling proved to be an excellent way of catching her dinner. It was smaller and more maneuverable than her bow, so she wasn't fighting against it to get a single shot off. Leather and stone, giving her the means to support herself on the journey.

Though she avoided contact with other people, she didn't always manage to evade them completely. She met shepherds and goatherds out with their flocks. These were less likely to fear her than average villagers, since they were more afraid of things like wolves. Even when they got close enough to see her horns and tail, they would still bid her hello. Their only disappointment was that she never seemed to know any news of the outside world, which she had not realized was currency in the middle of nowhere. It was a pleasant surprise to be considered so completely mundane.

One day, as summer was starting to really dig in, she came to a pond that had formed during the last of the spring floods and was still clinging to existence, though it was clearly drying up. The mud that bounded the water was cracked, and the plants seemed to reach in vain for the water. None of that was particularly important, given the time of year. What *was* important was that in the middle of the pond there stood a boy who looked to be only a little bit older than she was.

He was tall, and his skin was brown and sun-freckled in the summer heat. His hair was short, neatly framing his pointed ears. He was, for some reason, fully clothed, even though the water came up to his waist. He held his satchel above his head to keep it dry. He looked confused.

"Hello!" he said when he saw her. "How are you?"

"I'm fine," Doric replied carefully. "How are you?"

"Oh, you know," the boy said. "Wet."

"That happens in ponds," Doric pointed out.

"Yes, I was aware of that before I came in," the boy said.

Someone else might have asked him why, but Doric wasn't really interested in conversation. She'd come to the pond to refill her waterskin, but now she didn't want to. She had no idea how long he'd been standing there, and the pond wasn't that big.

"I'm Simon, by the way," the boy said. "I'm a sorcerer."

"Doric," Doric said, because even though she'd never met one, she'd heard that it always paid to be polite to sorcerers.

"You're a tiefling!" Simon said. "That's really neat."

A long pause stretched between them. Simon's bag was still above his head.

"Anyway, did you have plans for dinner?" Simon asked. "I was thinking about dinner."

"It's two hours after noon," Doric said.

Simon looked a bit crestfallen.

"So, that means afternoon tea or something?" he inquired.

"No," Doric said.

It wasn't like she couldn't refill her waterskin in the river. It was just more likely she'd get wet that way. She figured she had about two hours of water left if she was careful. She liked to hold some in reserve just in case, so she could probably make it farther, but there was no need to be incautious just because she'd met a strange boy in a pond.

"I'm heading out," Simon said. "I'm going north."

He started wading out of the pool, clothes cartoonishly ballooned and dripping with water. A frog leapt from one of his flooded pockets and back into the pond.

"I am . . . not," she said with a bewildered stare.

"Oh," Simon said. He narrowed his eyes as if he were really looking at her for the first time, focusing on her armor. Doric braced herself. "Are you a druid, then?" he said.

The question caught her off guard. It was the first time anyone had ever asked her. Liavaris had told her, Fenjor had assumed as much, and the spirit in the tree had been, well, a spirit in a tree, but still weird about it. The elves had accepted the declaration immediately, and none of the humans she'd met so far had cared.

"Yes," she said before the pause got too awkward.

Simon picked his way through the drying mud, his wet clothes running rivulets of water through the dirt.

"Well, then I actually have another question for you," he admitted with a sheepish slump of his shoulders. "There's a village called Willowdale just over that hill there." He gestured with both hands, the bag listing open as he moved it. "They're having a problem with their wells, something about their gardens not growing as well as they usually do in spring, and now it's almost too late to catch up. I was trying to help them."

"By standing in a pond." Doric lifted an eyebrow.

"I had planned to cast a spell," Simon told her with a sigh. "It did not work out. I'll be washing algae off myself for days."

"I can see that," Doric said.

She looked at the river and then at the sun, which was still high enough in the sky that she wasn't thinking about where she'd camp that night. Surely it wouldn't take too long to help a village and get back on her way. Plus, if she was being entirely honest, it was probably best to ask the locals for advice about the road ahead. The shepherds were fine, but their directions had already gotten her turned around twice.

"All right," Doric said. "Show me what the problem is."

Simon led the way back to Willowdale, talking cheerfully about all the things he had tried to do so far to fix the problem. She wasn't familiar with his techniques, knowing nothing about sorcery, but she appreciated that he kept trying. Before long, they came to the little hollow where the village sheltered from the winds.

This place was nothing like Helm's Hold, except that they both had houses and shops. Here, the houses were crammed together, and many of them were several stories high. It made sense if they needed protection from the weather, but Doric felt her skin crawl at the idea of so many people packed into such a small place. The wood elf tree village wasn't large, but it was spread out, and there was a whole forest around it. Here, there was nothing that freeing.

Simon walked to the center of the village, where a wide stone well stood in the middle of a modest public square. A small crowd came out to see him, and none of them looked particularly happy about it.

"They're not thrilled that nothing I did helped," Simon whispered loudly.

Doric was on her guard. She had thought Simon would be a useful ally in the village, which was one of the reasons she had agreed to come and help a bunch of random humans. If they didn't like him, they definitely wouldn't like her. Several of them were eyeing her already, and there was no mistaking their expressions when they saw her horns and tail. She wanted to flee and leave them to their troubles.

"Are you back again?" asked an old woman with gray braids twisted around her head and puffs of flour on her apron. "I've had enough magic from you."

"I've brought help this time." Simon put his hands up defensively. "This is Doric."

"We can see her," said the old woman. "What are you supposed to do?"

Doric tried to make herself look as unthreatening as possible. She held up her hands so they could see she was unarmed and spoke in a voice like the one Torrieth used when she was trying to con her cousins out of sweets.

"I know I am a stranger to you," she said, her distrust of humans at war with her desire to get out of this situation as peaceably as possible. "But I was raised by wood elves in the Neverwinter Wood. I would offer you the knowledge I gained from them. Wells are easy for them to handle."

There was some grumbling from the assembled humans, but the old woman silenced them with a glare.

"I suppose you can't make it any worse," she said. "Go ahead and take a look around."

She hustled the other villagers away from the well while Doric went to take a closer look at it. Simon came to stand beside her, just outside what she would have deemed too close.

"Can you really fix it?" he asked quietly.

"I can try," she told him.

She examined the stonework of the low wall that surrounded the well, poking at the mortar. Some of it flaked away at her touch, and she leaned over to smell it. She looked up, hoping that the old woman was still within earshot.

"Excuse me," Doric called out. The old woman took a few steps closer. "Do you know how old the stonework here is?"

"My parents built it when I was a girl," the old woman said. "So it's old."

"It's very solidly made," Doric said. "But over time, the water has washed the mortar out from between the stones. The lime in the mortar went into the well and changed the water. It will fix itself eventually, especially if you get a lot of rain this summer, but I would recommend re-laying the stonework. If you could do it without mortar, that would be best."

The old woman looked at her with grudging respect.

"It's always something simple, isn't it," she said. "And a stranger had to come and tell us."

"My guardian always told me that fresh eyes were helpful," Doric said. "Though now that I think about it, that was usually when she wanted me to finish a task she wasn't enjoying."

The old woman gave a bark of laughter. None of the villagers behind her looked amused, though. They were still glaring at Simon.

"We can't offer you much," the old woman said. "But you have my thanks."

"I do have a question for you," Doric said. Then she remembered her waterskin. "And if I could refill my water, that would be nice. The water is perfectly safe to drink, just not very good for plants right now."

The old woman lowered the bucket herself, and Doric worked quickly. She'd been helpful, but the mood in the village was still tense. She didn't want to linger any more than she had to.

"I am hoping you can tell me if there are any druids in the area," Doric said. She didn't exactly keep her voice down, but she definitely spoke more quietly than she had before. "I'm looking to reach the Emerald Enclave, somewhere in Ardeep Forest."

"None around here," the old woman said. "But if you go a bit farther south, the river widens out enough that they have barges and boats to sail up and down it. Those people hear more news than we do, on account of how they travel more. They might be able to help you."

"Thank you," Doric said with an earnest bob of her head.

After a few more words of farewell, Doric was on her way. It was only when she passed the last house and came out of the hollow that she realized Simon was still with her.

"You didn't even use a spell," he said, almost like an accusation.

"I didn't need one," Doric said. She left out the part where she didn't *know* one. "Sometimes you can just fix things the normal way."

Simon seemed to consider it for a moment and then shrugged his acceptance.

"You're sure it's too early for dinner?" he asked. His smile was nice enough, she supposed.

"Yes," she said.

"It was worth a shot," Simon said. He swung his satchel over one shoulder so that the bag fell at his hip and offered a friendly wave. "I'll see you around, Doric."

Having walked as far as she had, Doric found that thought extremely unlikely.

CHAPTER 8

As the old woman had said, the river widened out as Doric went south. The warming air was drying the mud on the riverbank, which made the walk more pleasant every day. Where the river was wide enough for barges to fit, there was a small town. Doric had an argument with herself about whether she should put her hood up before she went in search of information, but the problem solved itself when the sky opened up and it started to rain.

No one looked at her twice as she made her way down the street. She had come into town at the north end, and the boats were all docked at the south. If she wanted to talk to a traveler, it seemed the best place to start. Plus, there was a better chance of talking to someone outside, which meant keeping her hood up. Doric hated it, but the distrusting stares from the villagers she'd helped were at the front of her mind. These new people had no reason to help her. She had to use every advantage she could, even if it was distasteful.

The docks were crawling with humans. Once Doric looked more closely, she saw that there was no shortage of dwarves, dragonborn, and orcs, but the humans always attracted her attention first. Now that she was here, she had no idea how to approach people. Simply walking up to someone and asking about druids seemed impractical. As she watched the ebb and flow of the people who worked on the docks, one figure drew her gaze.

He was old, she was pretty sure. His forehead was weathered, but from this distance she couldn't tell much about him. What held her attention was that he was sitting down. Everyone else was bustling about like they had a place to be. This person might be easier to talk to.

As she made her way over to him, she realized he was working. A basket of fish sat beside him on the dock, and he was methodically cleaning them, his bright fillet knife flashing even in the gloom of the rain. He seemed unbothered by the water falling from the sky, and Doric wondered how much bad weather he had seen in his life. As she got closer to him, she was able to tell more about his appearance. He was a stout human with a round face and an impressive gray mustache.

"Excuse me," she said when she was close enough that he'd be able to hear her. "I'm sorry to interrupt, but I was hoping to ask you a few questions?"

"Ask away," the fisherman said. He spoke with a lilting accent that Doric had never heard before, his words dancing like whitecaps on a wind-tossed sea. She wondered what had brought him to this river. "I don't need to look at you to talk, and the fish don't mind."

Doric supposed they didn't.

"Have you heard of any druids in the area?" Doric asked. "Or know anything about Ardeep Forest?"

The knife flashed, and silver scales joined the rain in falling onto the dock. A second basket of cleaned fish sat on the man's other side, and Doric was impressed by how much of his catch was already in it.

"You know, I think there was talk of something like that a few months back," the fisherman said. His movements didn't slow. "A town south of here, up the Dessarin River near the Ardeep Forest. They were having trouble with wolves, and some druids stepped in to stop them from wiping out the predators to protect their sheep."

"Do you know how I would get there?" Doric asked. That sounded perfect, exactly the sort of druid stuff she was looking for. Could these be the same druids that Sunmuir had trained with?

"I can take you past Waterdeep to the mouth of the Dessarin River—if you can pay," the fisherman said. "When I'm not scaling fish for market, I sail the soundest ship on the river or sea. It's that one over there."

The vessel he pointed at looked sturdy enough,

though Doric knew nothing about shipbuilding. When she looked back, she realized that the fisherman had stopped working and was staring straight at her. His gaze dropped to where her tail hung, just visible beneath her cloak.

Several of the books that Doric had read had told her that captains tended to be a superstitious lot. Doric braced herself for a change in his demeanor, certain that he would balk at the idea of transporting a tiefling.

"You don't need special food, do you?" he asked. "Had a harengon a few weeks ago that wouldn't eat anything without parsley for decoration. She was kind of a pain."

"I'll eat anything," Doric said. She let the captain believe that meant food, and not the entire craft. If he didn't know all the details about what being a tiefling meant, she was in no hurry to educate him.

"I'll take half the pay now, the rest when we get there," he said. "We leave tomorrow at first light. My name is Dartha, by the way."

"Your crew won't mind?" Doric asked.

"Not if they want to get paid," Dartha said. "I don't care if you're an actual demon as long as you have the fee. At worst, you're only half a demon, and most of the stories about tieflings are hogwash anyway."

"Thank you," Doric said.

"First light," Dartha repeated. "We won't wait for you."

"I'll be here," Doric said.

It took Doric about five minutes to decide that boats were definitely better than walking.

"It's called a ship," Dartha told her when she said as much. "You can tell because I'm a captain and everyone has to do what I say. Boats are more of a committee thing."

Doric filed that away for future reference and went back to hanging off the ropes that bound the sail to the mast. The ship had only the one mast, and the mast had only one sail. They didn't really need it for the river, because of the current, but Captain Dartha was not the sort to waste time if he didn't have to, and they'd definitely need it on the sea. The crew were up and down the ropes and ladders all day, changing the set of the sail with the wind and making sure everything was in good condition. This part of summer was almost always fair weather, Dartha told her, but there were autumn storms coming, even in the protected waters near the coast, and they had to be sure the ship was always in top shape so they'd be ready.

Doric coiled rope for the sailors, mostly to keep busy. They didn't really need her help, but she would much rather sit on the deck than wait in her cramped cabin, and she wasn't the sort to be idle when other people were working. The sailors talked almost constantly as they sailed, and even though they didn't talk to her, they didn't mind her listening. They shared their captain's tolerance of her to a point. No one said anything, and no one treated her poorly, but it was easier for everyone if she kept her distance and didn't interfere with their labor.

"Can you hang on that thing?" one of the younger crew members asked her, pointing to her tail. His name was Adar, and he peppered everyone with endless questions. Doric appreciated that, because it meant she learned a lot without actually having to talk to anyone. "You can move it around and stuff, but does it bear your weight?"

Doric had never tried, but as soon as the question was asked, she decided she might as well find out.

They picked a spot over the bow where Doric wouldn't fall as far because the deck below was raised, and also there were fewer people working in the front of the ship. There was a small, roofed pen in the bow for when Dartha transported livestock, and a rope had been strung between it and the forecastle for laundry. It wasn't entirely sturdy, but it would do.

"Okay," she said, inching out onto the pen while keeping hold of the rope.

She wound her tail around the rope three times, locking the flared end in place in the coils. Then she eased herself off the pen, lowering herself until her arms reached their limit.

"Come on, then," said Adar.

"You try it," Doric grumbled, but she gamely let go.

The important thing was that her tail held. She fell only a couple of feet before it caught her weight, jerking her up a bit and holding steady as she twisted like a fish on the end of a line. The part she hadn't counted on was that it *hurt*.

"OW," she said, then added a few of the words the sailors had taught her to the end of her exclamation.

Adar almost fell over laughing.

"I will pull every hair from your head," Doric said.

She was still swinging, but now that the movement was less, it didn't hurt quite so much. Maybe this was more of a lifting thing than a falling thing.

"Do you need help down?" Adar asked, getting ahold of himself.

"No, I've got it," Doric said.

She worked the end of her tail free, and the rest of it unwound from the rope. She landed heavily on the deck, but she landed on her feet.

"That was both the funniest and most interesting thing I've ever seen," Dartha said. Doric had not realized he'd been watching and felt a little mortified. Still, the captain wasn't one to feign sincerity for a moment, and she found it touching. "You might want to practice a bit more if you want to make a go of it, though."

"I'm good, thanks," Doric said. She resisted the urge to rub her behind. "I think I'll go to my cabin, actually. I'm feeling a little tired."

In her cabin, Doric spent a few minutes picking things up and moving them around with her tail to make sure she hadn't injured it, but it seemed like it was fine. She thought about Adar, laughing at her in the good way, and the way Dartha thought about things that scared other people. She started to laugh, too, remembering how it felt to swing from the rope. She'd have to remember it so that she could tell Torrieth.

THE REST OF the voyage passed uneventfully. The river ran into the sea, but the small ship stuck close to the coastline, docking here or there to let off a passenger or trade for food. Soon, the wide mouth of the Dessarin River came into view, and Doric knew her time on the ship was ended.

Captain Dartha was reluctant to leave her on the riverbank by herself, even though Doric assured him she would be fine. In the end, he poled her to shore on the little raft that the ship used to make landfall without a pier, offering advice about what she might find in the area the whole time. He told her to steer clear of Waterdeep, citing that, in his opinion, the crowded city failed to live up to the nickname "The City of Splendors." He'd much rather have water beneath his feet anyway. Mostly he talked about the village to the east that had needed the druids' intervention with the wolves, but Doric listened to all of it. One never knew when information would come in handy.

By now, Doric had been traveling south for almost three weeks. Since she had spent the last few days moving more quickly than she could walking, she had covered a great deal of ground. It was hotter here, though not as warm as it got in the Neverwinter Wood, and summer was clearly further along than it had been in the north. There were rolling hills and plowed fields aplenty. There were also more signs of habitation, from crofter cabins to full-sized towns. The ship hadn't stopped at any of them, but Doric guessed that when Dartha wasn't transporting passengers or fishing, he could call at each town to see if there was any freight. It would be an interesting sort of life, traveling up and down the rivers of the Sword Coast, just enough moving around to keep a person interested without being very dangerous. It wasn't for her, but Doric could see the attraction of it.

"And don't stuff catfish with sweet berries," Dartha finished as the raft gently scraped the bottom of the river near the bank. "They need something savory, like spinach or cheese."

"I will keep that in mind," Doric said, struggling to keep a straight face.

"Look," said Dartha, "I know you made it this far mostly on your own and all that, but people aren't meant to be all by themselves. Some druids disappear entirely, gone off into the woods to meditate or something. Don't do that. You've got people, from what you've told me, and that's better than sitting on some tree stump by yourself."

Doric wanted nothing more than to return to the wood elves, and she feared nothing more than the idea that they wouldn't take her back. Running into the forest would be easy. From her traveling and training, she knew she could get by, but Dartha had a point.

"Thank you, Captain," she said.

Doric counted the second half of her fare into his palm, and he accepted it with a smile. He held out his other hand to steady her while she jumped from the raft to the bank. It was a surprise to touch someone, especially a human, but Doric did it without thinking about it. The push was enough that she made it all the way to the bank without getting her feet wet. When she looked back, Dartha wasn't staring at his hand like he expected it to be burnt or something. He was simply holding her bag, ready to throw it to her.

"You may not need me again," he said, "given the potential for flying and other druid things, but if you do need a ship, come down and check for me. I'm in and out with the herb harvests."

"Thank you. I will," Doric said.

She waved to the sailors, who were watching her departure with mixed levels of relief, and pulled her bag up on her shoulder. As soon as Captain Dartha was back on board, the ship weighed anchor and continued its way south. They would pick up cargo somewhere else before beginning the return trip northward. Doric checked the angle of the sun to get her bearings and then turned away from the river.

Her boots were already broken in from the first part of her journey, and as Doric crossed the uneven fields, she was extra glad of it. The meadows were a little bit easier, but if she was in a plowed field, she tried to stay in a furrow and away from the sprouting crops. There wasn't a road or path that she could find, but she didn't want to show up at the village asking for help having trampled all over their spring sowing. It took concentration to pick her way through, so she got quite close to the village before she realized she was there.

Behind the village stood a pine forest. The wind was blowing towards her, and Doric could already smell the distinctive trees. The Emerald Enclave was undoubtedly in the forest somewhere. From what Captain Dartha had said, the druids had come to prevent the people from killing wolves. That didn't make it sound like the villagers would have any great love for the druids, and Doric thought that, combined with their automatic distrust of her appearance, they weren't likely to help her find them. She could come back to the village later if she needed to. Right now, it made more sense to go around it and see if she could find the druid camp right away.

It was a relief to be back under the eaves of a forest again. Even though the Neverwinter Wood tended to have mostly oak and ash trees, broad-leaved and whispering in the wind, the pine and cedar trees were familiar enough. Doric trailed her fingertips over the bark and then laughed at her own sentimentality. She was going to have to focus if she wanted to find the druids, not spend her time looking at trees.

She made her way deeper into the forest. The ground was covered with low-lying shrubs and sedges, but it wasn't too difficult to walk through. There were hummocks and deadfalls, but she could scramble over most of them. She could hear birds in the branches above her, but she hadn't seen any animals yet. There were probably bears here if there were wolves. She kept an eye out, but she didn't think she was in any danger.

The signs were so faint she almost missed them, but eventually Doric found a game trail that was just a little too straight to have been made by a deer. She followed it and saw evidence of berry bushes that had been prudently harvested, as well as mushroom growths with half the bells missing. Someone had been foraging with the intent to support regrowth, carefully limiting how much they took so that there would be enough to grow back next year. It certainly seemed like a very druid thing to do.

Doric smelled the faintest amount of smoke on the wind and continued in that direction. The trail led that way, and smoke was a good indication of habitation in a forest that was still too wet for fire season. She did not try to move quietly, like she would do if she were hunting. She didn't want to sneak up on anyone.

With no warning, two green-cloaked figures stepped out from behind pine trees on opposite sides of the path. Both had arrows on their strings, though neither of them was yet at full draw. Doric froze immediately, raising her hands to show that they had nothing to fear from her. One of the figures lowered their bow, but the other didn't move.

"Tiefling?" The first ranger tilted his head. He sounded more surprised and curious than afraid. "We don't get many of you."

"What is your business here?" the second demanded, scowling down her arrow. "Why have you come so far into the forest?"

"I'm a druid," Doric said after clearing her throat. "Or at least I would like to be."

"Go on." The first ranger gestured with his wrist as he spoke.

"I'm from the Neverwinter Wood," Doric explained. "I grew up with the wood elves there. They don't have any druids who could teach me, but one of their own was trained by the Emerald Enclave, so I came here looking for them. For you?"

The second ranger lowered her bow and placed the arrow back in the quiver on the belt at her waist.

"You found us." She clicked her tongue. "Not many can without guidance."

Now that she was no longer held at arrowpoint, Doric took a closer look at the rangers. The first was a half-elf, and the second appeared human. They'd reacted more to her being in the woods than anything. They were probably used to people being in the forest for the wrong reasons. Doric's mind wandered back to the intruders logging in the Neverwinter Wood.

"I would like to learn how to be a druid," Doric said with greater composure. "If there is no one here who can teach me, could you maybe give me directions to someone who could?"

The two rangers exchanged a look.

"We don't make those kinds of decisions," said the woman. "But I can take you to someone who can."

The woman set off briskly through the forest. Doric kept up, even though she was already tired from walking all day. She followed the guard until they came to a clearing in the forest where the trees didn't block out the sky. It was big enough for two large buildings, several smaller outbuildings, and a few clusters of tents. There were gardens and what appeared to be a training arena. Everywhere Doric looked, she saw people of all races. Some of them were clearly druids. Others were rangers like the two she'd already met, and there were even some barbarians tending to companion dogs and hawks. She'd known the Enclave wasn't just druids, but seeing this many people at the same time was still a bit unexpected.

"Palanus," said the ranger. "We have a visitor."

A burly half-orc detached themself from the crowd. From their size, Doric might have assumed they were one of the barbarians, but it was clear as soon as they turned around that they were not. They stood tall and upright, with a pile of braids gathered into a ponytail and their head shaved underneath and over their ears. Their eyes were gray like oncoming thunderheads but had such intensity that a storm might be made self-conscious by comparison.

"All the way from the Neverwinter Wood," the ranger continued. "Clearly she was pretty determined to find us."

Palanus stopped in front of Doric and looked down at her. Doric tried to meet their gaze, but it was difficult to hold. She was suddenly conscious of every tear in her tunic and every scuff mark on her boots from her travels.

"You wish to be a druid?" they asked simply.

"I think I am one," Doric said, mustering up her courage. "I just need training."

"An interesting way to look at it," Palanus mused. "I have several students already. One more does not make that much of a difference to me, but some of them have been here for a few months already. You will have to work hard to catch up."

"I am good at working hard," Doric said. "I was training to be a ranger before, when I was still with the wood elves in the Neverwinter Wood. I know it's not the same thing, but it's a place to start."

"Indeed," Palanus said. "One must wonder, though, why you want to be trained as a druid so badly?"

Doric flushed and looked down. It was hard to admit out loud, but she had a feeling that the truth would get her very far here.

"I tried to protect a friend from a bear that was driven from its range. I almost calmed it down, but I couldn't help but empathize with its anger. It broke away from me, and my friend got hurt," she said.

"You wish to better serve your friends?" Palanus inquired. "Druids do not prioritize one person over another. All are equal in nature, and nature's balance must be your main concern."

Doric bit her lip and considered her next words.

"The wood elves haven't had a druid live amongst them for a long time," she said. "I had hoped that if I learned to understand, I could return to them and be more useful."

"That sounds like you wish to serve yourself," Palanus said. Their voice was strangely gentle. They weren't judging Doric, merely guiding her towards the right path. "Druids must be content knowing that those around them might never appreciate their work."

Doric blew out a breath, hoping that she didn't look as frustrated as she felt. She understood that what she was asking for was a privilege. She had no idea how to convince them she was worth it.

"On my way here, I passed a village," she said after a long moment. "I didn't know them, and they didn't trust me, because I am a tiefling." Doric couldn't miss the flash of anger in Palanus's eyes. Encouraged, she barreled forward with her story. "There was something wrong with their well. The water wasn't helping their gardens grow the way that it usually did. I don't know any spells or magic, but when I looked at the well, I knew that there was too much lime in the water, seeped in from the mortar they'd used when they built it. I told them, and I suggested how to fix it. The well won't be contaminated anymore."

"And how will that help nature?" Palanus asked. There was genuine warmth in their voice for the first time.

"They won't have to track down to the river," Doric said. "That would cause the ground to be muddy, and the soil could be swept downstream. Oh, and they won't have to dig irrigation channels from the river to the town! They won't have to divert the water, and everything will stay as it is."

There was a moment of silence that stretched out beyond measure.

"I recognize that armor. Sunmuir was a teacher of mine, once upon a time. I assume anyone who inherited it wouldn't come all this way for nothing." Palanus smiled warmly. "You have a lot to learn. A druid's life is one of knowledge and labor, but you seem fit to the task. Welcome to the Emerald Enclave."

LATER, SHE WOULD LEARN THAT THERE WERE other forests that definitely would have been worse. For now, she knew only that trees block the sunlight, that food runs out easily, and that she was going to have to teach herself a lot of things very quickly if she was going to survive.

The Neverwinter Wood stretched out around her, full of animals she hadn't seen and plants she didn't understand. She knew that she could eat tree bark now, but she found that berries and moss were more palatable. The water was clear, and she knew to wash downstream of where she drank. For the first time in her life, she was free to make all the noise she wanted without worrying that she might disturb those below.

The space was what really got to her. Her world had been so small for so long, with just one window to look out on things that were more interesting. Now the interesting things were all around her, and she was drawn to them. She held green leaves from the top of broad-branched trees and thought about how different they were from the dried brown leaves that clustered around the trunk. She counted the fish in the pond where she bathed, marveling as a new generation spawned before her eyes. She heard the rustle of squirrels and rabbits and owls, and knew immediately which of them she had the most in common with.

She learned to hunt from watching the owl, her eyes wide in the dark as the ghostly shape flew from tree to tree. She learned to be quiet. She learned to be quick. She learned that she needed to chew but that she didn't need to cook her food on her meager fire first. She learned that meat and bone were really all the same to her and that viscera went down just as easily. She preferred to keep that part of eating in the dark, and then she could wash her clothes at first light.

Before that, though, she was suffering. She was hungrier than she had ever been in the attic, and she had no idea how to get the food she needed. The animals mystified her, disappearing into the brush as soon as she found them. She did what she could with fennel and roots, but it wasn't enough. Soon, she was so hungry that walking around hurt, and she leaned back against a tree while the sun set, trying to save her energy.

The cold, hard emptiness that was her belly made it hard to think, but at least the air was

warm. She felt the wind against her cheek, ruf-
fling her hair around her horns. Her tail twitched
on the ground beside her, unwilling to give up.
She was tired, and she was miserable—and that
was when she looked up and saw the owl.

She didn't know that snowy owls were rare
in these particular woods, though when she
eventually thought about it, the reason was obvious. All she knew was that the creature was
the most beautiful thing she'd ever seen, white
wings spread wide against the darkening sky.
The owl ignored her and hopped ahead from
branch to branch, following something she
couldn't sense.

It took everything she had left to stand, but
she hauled herself to her feet. She leaned against
each tree as she followed the owl through the
trunks. It pulled her along through curiosity
and compulsion, and even though she didn't
know the question, she longed to find out the
answer.

Eventually the owl stilled. The woods got
even more quiet. She held her breath as the owl
slowly spread its silent wings and kept holding it
as the owl plummeted to the forest floor, flaring
feathers at the last minute to pull up with a
squirrel, already past struggling, in its talons.

She had thought that power was a ladder to
the loft, the rope on which the bread basket
came up, the ability to look at a daughter and

poison her drink. She learned now that power could be other things, too. The ability to feed yourself. The ability to hunt. She had never eaten squirrel, but as she watched the owl throw its head back and down the rodent in large chunks, she decided that it was probably a good place to start.

She had picked every berry and fiddlehead in walking distance by the time she finally landed her first squirrel. It took a tenday of nights watching the owl, trying to feel what it felt and see what it saw, until she figured it out. When she caught herself a dinner that would sustain her longer than any foraged handful ever could, she didn't hesitate to kill it.

Death for life wasn't something she had thought about before, but when she was faced with it, her survival became the most important thing. She held the still-warm creature in her hands, and quietly thanked the squirrel before she bit, teeth tearing off chunks of fur and meat. She chewed everything before she gulped it down. She wasted nothing, just like the owl. She wouldn't throw up pellets later, but her body would digest everything it could.

She didn't remember the way the owl watched her. She didn't think it was strange at the time, because she didn't know that wild animals usually avoided people.

She didn't know that the owl had taught her

on purpose, waiting patiently while she put the pieces together and hooting triumphantly as she made her first kill.

By the time she killed her second squirrel, the owl had moved on. She would not think about it for years, but she decided that she preferred rabbit almost immediately.

CHAPTER 9

There were seven young druid hopefuls in the circle
of initiates: two humans, an elf, a halfling, a firbolg,
and an air genasi. Plus one tiefling. Doric didn't need
anyone to tell her that it was a strange group. She had
heard of all these kinds of people, but she had never
imagined seeing all of them together at the same time.
Palanus directed her over to them but didn't provide any
further instruction before they turned back to talk to
another member of the Enclave who seemed to have a
pressing question. The Emerald Enclave accepted anyone who would uphold its ideals.

"How did you get here?" the elf boy asked.

"I walked," Doric said. "Until I needed a boat, of course."

"I can't believe you managed to find the camp on your own," the human boy said. "The rest of us had to be brought in."

"I guess I'm used to doing things on my own," said Doric. She was almost daring him to ask why.

"Leave it alone," said the second human, a girl. "We're all here, and we've all been accepted. There's no reason to be an ass about it."

The boy glared at her, a hint of jealousy barely contained behind his eyes. Doric swallowed a smile.

"I'm Cassa," said the girl. She had dark brown skin and straight black hair. "What's your name?"

"Doric." Doric bobbed her head.

Cassa looked expectantly at the others, and they eventually gave up their names as well. The human boy was Leander. He was pale like Doric, but his hair was almost as dark as Cassa's. The elf was named Remigold. He mostly resembled the elves that Doric had grown up with, except his skin was closer to golden than copper, and he had curly hair and an open face. The air genasi was Mistral. He was whipcord thin with blue skin and bright white hair. Beside him, the halfling, Gragwen, looked even smaller, though it was plain from her wide smile and the mischief in her eyes that she was not to be overlooked. Jowenys, the firbolg, seemed to be the most comfortable around Doric. Her bright red hair made her gray skin shine in the dappled light under the trees.

Doric committed each name to memory. It was clear

they were going to be with one another for a while, and she liked knowing what to call people. She'd met all the elves in her clan at the same time, too, and it had been very overwhelming. At least there were only six new names to learn here.

"I'm glad there will be someone else to help with the hunting," Jowenys said. She was tall and broad, usual for a firbolg, and carried a staff like she knew how to use it.

"You like hunting?" Cassa asked.

"Not every day," Jowenys said. "It's just lonely when you have to do it alone all the time."

"Jowenys and I got here the day after the last full moon," Remigold said by way of explanation. "We've all been trying our hands at as much as we can."

"I'm excited to be here," Doric said. She was surprised by how easy it was to talk with everyone. Their shared cause and forced proximity probably had a lot to do with it. "But I understand not wanting to spend all your time doing work alone for other people."

"You get used to it," Mistral said. "A lot of being a druid is helping other people."

"Only if you're doing it wrong," Leander said. "If you're doing it right, you get to be a wolf."

"Have you Wild Shaped already?" Jowenys asked. She sounded excited and awed. "Turned into an animal and all that?"

Leander smirked and leaned on one foot, shifting his shoulders like he was looking down on Jowenys, even though she was at least six inches taller than he was.

"Of course he hasn't," Cassa said deflatingly. "We've only been here a month." Leander's confident grin cracked.

Jowenys giggled, a sound like water over rocks. It reminded Doric of how Liavaris laughed. Leander crossed his arms and glared at all of them.

"Well, you can't either," he said. "And we've had the longest time to learn."

"Shut up, Leander," Cassa said. "I'm exhausted, and I didn't walk all the way here tonight. Let's just go back to the cabin so Doric can rest."

"And get what rest we can before our revered elders remember that we're here to learn and wake us up to teach us something," Mistral added.

Palanus and other important-looking druids had withdrawn to the other end of the clearing once Doric had been welcomed. They seemed to be talking amongst themselves quite heatedly, gesticulating wildly so that their sleeves flapped in the air and their various accessories clattered against one another. There were no raised voices, but the tension was obvious, and at least one of them had already stormed off.

"Members of the Emerald Enclave are only allowed to disagree with each other in official gathering spaces," Cassa explained. "It's one of the rules."

"They seem to be enjoying themselves," Mistral said.

The young druids made their way across the clearing to a long stone building with a thatched roof. Doric followed the others quietly. Her pack was digging into her shoulder uncomfortably. She hadn't set it down in hours, and she couldn't wait to rest for a bit.

The cabin was built in the lee of a small rise in the ground that had been cut so that the floors inside would be level without sacrificing any height in the walls. It was much bigger than the word "cabin" suggested. Like the other buildings in the clearing, it was built of stone and reinforced with living wood. Doric had no idea how the druids were able to make trees grow exactly where they wanted them to in a clearing, but she was sure that would be part of their coming lessons. The door was made of cut wood, however, and swung on hinges. Not everything the druids did was entirely mystical, it seemed.

The cabin was divided into three living spaces, plus a kitchen that Doric couldn't see into. There was a great room with a long dining table and a huge fireplace with plenty of seats around it; the study, where books and strange objects lined the shelves; and the bedrooms. These were small and tucked at the back, though each had a window and a view of green. Doric had been expecting a small cot, but what she found were two beds stacked on top of each other, living tree trunks serving as bedposts for both beds at once. Jowenys had followed her into the room.

"Well," Jowenys started. "I don't suppose you snore?"

"I don't think so," Doric said. She appreciated the other girl's forthright attitude.

"That's fine," Jowenys said. "I've already taken the top."

Jowenys heaved herself up to the top bunk. The bed didn't move as she did, which made Doric feel better about sleeping underneath. She put her bag down be-

side the lower bunk and sat down. There was plenty of
room for her to sit up straight without her horns grazing the bottom of the bed above.

"So Leander's pretty full of himself, eh?" Jowenys
said. "But Cassa's nice. Did you have to travel far to get
here?"

"I lived with wood elves," Doric said. "In the Neverwinter Wood."

"That *is* a long ways off." Jowenys sounded concerned. "You came alone?"

"My friends from the elf clan brought me as far as
they could," Doric said. "They tried to train me as a
ranger, so I can mostly take care of myself."

Jowenys stuck her head over the side of the bed, re-
garding Doric from upside down like it was a totally
normal way of looking at a person.

"If you say so," Jowenys said.

She slumped back on the mattress above, disappearing from view. Doric took off her boots and kicked her
feet up on the bed, resting her head on the pillow for a
moment before rolling onto her side to take the pressure
off her tail. No mattress was that soft.

"I have approximately a million questions," Jowenys
said. She yawned so widely her jaw cracked. "But we've
got plenty of time, and I'm going to fall asleep and forget anything you tell me anyway. Good night, Doric."

"Good night," Doric said.

True to her word, Jowenys fell asleep almost immediately. And she did snore, but it was a very delicate
sound. It reminded Doric of a purring cat.

Doric was tired, too, but she couldn't sleep quite yet.

She was buzzing with the excitement of finally having reached her goal. Not only had she found a branch of the Emerald Enclave, but she had also found a teacher. Palanus seemed a little intense, but they were in charge of a bunch of trainees. Fenjor got like that every time there was a new crop of rangers to teach. The other young druids seemed at least unbothered by her. She could win them over or ignore them, whatever she decided. They didn't know her past, and if she worked hard, she could control her future along with her new druid powers—a task that was finally starting to feel enticing instead of obligatory.

Wild Shape. As soon as she'd heard the words, she had felt an immediate interest. She liked learning about plants and water and that sort of thing, but the part of nature that moved and breathed and hunted appealed to her even more. She wanted to know what it would be like to be a wolf, a deer, a lynx. Even domestic animals like horses and house cats would be interesting.

Once again, she recalled the deeply buried memory of the snowy owl she had seen in the Neverwinter Wood when she was small. At the time, she hadn't thought it was strange. She hadn't known that owls were shy and that snowy owls preferred to stay where it actually snowed. She had been entranced by its silent wings and the power of its talons. And now she might actually be able to turn into one. Someday. If she practiced. She didn't know what sorts of skills she would have to practice to change from tiefling to creature and back again, but she wanted to learn.

That was why she was here, though. It wasn't enough

to have a connection to nature. She had to learn how to use it. How to work alongside it. Then, when she had learned to control her abilities, and would no longer intimidate anyone, she would return to her clan of elves in the Neverwinter Wood. By then, the human logging problem would have either grown as she feared or disappeared as Marlion suspected, and in either case, she'd be a druid, and she'd be able to help with whatever came next. Torrieth would be a true ranger by then, too. Together, they would be a force to be reckoned with.

But that was far away for now. Doric didn't even know simple spells yet. She would have to study hard.

"I can hear you thinking," Jowenys said. "And I know neither of us knows that spell yet."

Doric hadn't even noticed that the snoring had stopped.

"I'm sorry," Doric said. "Did I wake you?"

"No," Jowenys said. "I was craving a midnight snack, and I thought I'd share."

She swung down from the upper bunk and padded over to a rough wooden trunk. Jowenys rummaged through its contents until she raised a jar with a triumphant hum.

"I brought some fresh honeycomb from home." Jowenys held the jar out to Doric. "My clan takes care of some wild beehives. I heard familiar food helps with homesickness. Go on, try some."

Doric gingerly took the jar and opened it. There were four decent-sized pieces left, but it still wasn't a lot. "Are you sure you're okay sharing this with me? I don't want to take your food."

"You're not taking it from me if I'm offering." Jowenys fished a dripping piece of honeycomb out of the jar and popped it in her mouth, then grinned from ear to ear as she started to chew the wax.

Doric took the smallest piece of the remaining three and bit down on the delicate beeswax. The amber honey within was so sweet and fragrant that it was almost intoxicating. For a fleeting moment, it tasted like breakfast with Liavaris.

Emotion welled in Doric's throat, and she swallowed it down with the honey. "Thank you, Jowenys. It's really good."

"Isn't it?" Jowenys swung herself back up onto her bunk and flopped against her pillows. "Definitely the best way to finish off the day. Sleep well, Doric."

Doric's eyelids grew heavy as she listened to Jowenys's breathing grow steady and her purr-like snore rumble softly again. It seemed that now, across many lands and rivers, she had two friends.

CHAPTER 10

The first surprise of Doric's day came at breakfast. They all ate together, and Doric had been fully prepared to eat whatever was set in front of her, but when she arrived at the table, she saw that it was piled high with all kinds of incredible-smelling food. There were bowls of oatmeal, dotted with honey and partridgeberries, and plates with eggs and toast waiting for them. There were even little jars of preserves, each with a delicate spoon resting on the lid, and a fat pat of butter in a small dish.

Doric took a seat by Jowenys and looked down at her plate. The porridge might have been made from Neverwinter wildgrains. It looked and smelled like home, which was always a good way to start the day. Doric picked up one of the spoons, added a bit of orange jam to her bowl, and dug in.

"Ah, you've all begun. Excellent," a voice boomed from the kitchen. There was a brief clattering noise, and then someone backed out of the swinging door because his hands were full. "I hope everything is to your liking. I hate assuming you all eat the same things, but breakfast is better as a buffet in any case."

The cook was a tiefling. He was much taller than any of them, the tips of his horns almost grazing the ceiling. His skin was dark red, and his triangular face seemed to pull his lips towards his ears, revealing an earnest grin with pointed teeth. His tail was thick and long enough that it would have dragged on the floor, except he was using it to carry a floral tea towel that matched the apron he wore around his waist.

"I'm going to take your awed silence as a yes," he said. He turned to Doric. "What about you? I knew I should have fried up that bacon. Newcomers always need more protein."

"It's . . . fine," Doric said with a waver in her tone. Even to her own ears, her voice sounded far away. For the first time in her life, she was looking at someone who looked like her, and all she could do was stare. "Everything looks . . . very delicious."

The cook immediately sat down across from her. Doric knew it was rude, but she couldn't tear her eyes away from the tiefling. All her worries and doubts, all the little voices she'd struggled to hush when her mind was wandering, and there was a tiefling druid at her destination the whole time. She almost forgot to breathe.

"Have you met another tiefling before?" he asked.

"No," Doric said, her voice stronger. "Only me."

"We'll have a lot to talk about, then," he said. He smiled at her again. From the kitchen, something started whistling loudly. "They're playing my song!"

And then he walked back into the kitchen as though this sort of thing happened every morning.

The others immediately began a discussion of what they usually had for breakfast, and the conversation flowed on without Doric taking part. She ate her breakfast efficiently, scraping all the porridge out of her bowl and then mopping up the extra jam and honey with her toast.

"You're what my mother would call 'economical,'" Cassa said. "Though if you had a hound, I suppose it would have to give extra good calf-eyes."

"What did you eat on your way here?" asked Mistral.

"I am a good forager," Doric said. Their curiosity didn't sting, but Doric didn't entirely drop her guard. "I can eat a lot of things."

"Of course you're a good forager," Gragwen said, as if it were obvious. She tossed her frizzy blond hair out of her eyes. "You were taught by wood elves, and they're almost as good as us."

"It's one thing to say all that, but you don't know the first thing about being a druid," Leander scoffed. "It's a lot harder than just scrounging around for herbs or whatever."

"You certainly had nothing bad to say about the

herbs I scrounged up for my secret recipe mashed potatoes last night," said the cook, coming back in to collect their dishes. "We're all here to learn and improve ourselves. Some of us will clearly have more to do than others."

Doric watched as he swept around the table, his tail flicking behind him. She wanted to have that level of control one day. Maybe he would give her some advice.

"Now, you're all off to the garden for the morning," the tiefling said. "One of the others will find you there, and Palanus will find you when they are ready. They're your teacher, but they have other things to do as well. Try not to kill anything. Or each other."

"The gardens?" Leander complained. "I thought we were supposed to be learning about survival and self-reliance."

"What is more important to survival than food?" the tiefling proclaimed. "Particularly food that is reliable and plentiful enough to feed a large group. You've all learned to forage, but what about living as a community? There are limits to hunting and gathering."

Leander grumbled but trailed behind the others as they filed out, following Cassa, who clearly knew where she was going.

"What's your name?" Doric asked when it was just her and the cook left.

"Open," he said. "Pleased to make your acquaintance."

"I wasn't expecting another tiefling," Doric said. "Liavaris, my guardian, said that because there aren't many tieflings, we don't run into each other."

"I'm a people person," Open said. "Now skedaddle before that Leander comes up with a way to fill your garden clogs with snails."

"That's not a bad idea," Doric said. She had so many questions for him and wanted to stay, but she knew a dismissal when she heard one.

"You definitely did not hear it from me." Open winked.

Doric made her way to the garden, following the sound of everyone else talking. Jowenys was the most likely to be in control of the conversation, but she had no problem deferring to someone who knew more than she did. Right now, Gragwen was doing most of the talking. It seemed that her parents were tree farmers and had some skill at growing trees that could be used as part of living architecture.

"All right, then," said a new voice just as Doric came around the corner and saw the garden spread out in front of her. "My name is Kaliope, and I will be the one to guide you through the beginnings of your journey here."

She was a human woman, short and round, with ruddy cheeks and a scarf tied over her dark gray hair. She wore a linen apron with approximately a thousand pockets, all of which seemed to be filled with gardening tools of some kind. Doric had seen her the previous evening amongst the throng of druids, rangers, and barbarians but had avoided her as she normally avoided all humans. It didn't seem like that was going to be an option for very long, though. She was going to have to swallow her misgivings and listen. Kaliope waited until Doric had crossed all the way to the others, and then she began.

"As druids, we get our power from the raw force of nature," she said. "Some of you may venerate Silvanus, or another one of the nature gods. Each druid's relationship to nature is as unique as the druid themself. I see many unique aspiring druids here, and group work is more fun for me to watch, so I'm going to have you learn together."

Remigold made a noise that sounded suspiciously like a snort.

"As for why we're in the garden," Kaliope continued, "you will recall I said 'raw force of nature' just now. Our goal for today is to start small and get you accustomed to the slightly calmer version of nature one finds in a garden. I want you to go through all the rows, look at each plant, and see how it is growing. Try and feel the connection between you and it, two living things. And when you're ready to try, see if you can use that connection to encourage the plant to blossom or shed seeds."

It was a simple spell, and they couldn't do much damage with it, but it could be very useful, even with wild plants. Starting small made sense. Doric already knew that it was easier to control something small. That's why her parents had put her in the attic.

"That's it?" Leander said. "When I started, you made me haul water for an hour."

Kaliope gave him a measured glance, and he quailed, dropping his eyes to the ground. The rest of them split off in pairs, Leander attaching himself to a resigned Cassa and Mistral, and started working their way through the rows.

"I think this one is squash," Jowenys said, looking at a bulbous green vegetable that grew on the ground. "They come in all kinds of different shapes and colors."

Doric leaned over to touch one. She felt the flower that it had grown from, the water that it held inside its tough skin. Following Kaliope's instructions, she murmured a few words and kept her hand on the vegetable. It suddenly felt warm under her palm and grew ripe, but it remained stunted, small. Doric lifted the squash to examine it.

"You were able to shuffle the plant along," Kaliope said, appearing from nowhere. "But something seems wrong. What is it lacking?"

"I think maybe something in the soil," Doric said. "It's used up everything that it can reach. I've seen crops like this in the villages neighboring the wood elves sometimes. The plants were small and had a poor yield."

Jowenys set her hand on the side of the squash and tilted her head.

"I feel it," she said. "They're all like that."

"Plants take nutrients from the soil they grow in," Kaliope said. "Squash in particular are greedy. They're hearty and healthy, so people eat a lot of them, but they deplete the soil, so we have to let the ground rest between seasons of planting them."

"Will you feed the soil to restore it?" Doric asked.

"No," Kaliope said. "Next year we'll plant beans here

instead. That will set the soil right without us having to meddle too much."

Doric went down the other rows with Jowenys, feeling corn and tomatoes and some tubers that grew entirely below the ground, so she couldn't see what they looked like. Not all of them responded to her call, but when they did, they immediately seeded, blossomed, or ripened. There was a feeling of plenty, of a job well done, even if the soil was tiring and was almost ready for a break.

"Here," said Kaliope, handing them each a little shovel. "Dig into the earth and feel the difference in the soil as you go down."

The summer sun burned overhead, but Doric barely felt it. She forgot to care that Kaliope was human and that humans had hurt her in the past. It didn't seem to matter anymore. All of her attention was on the ground and the plants that were growing in it. They looked orderly, planted in rows and neatly tied to stakes, but they fought for life just as much as trees would in a forest. All of them wanted more, wanted higher, wanted up. And they strove for it with all the power they could muster. Doric felt that power course through her, and she felt strong.

"Now, fix this," Kaliope said, holding out a stake that had been snapped in two. "Feel where the ends should meet. Ask, and pull them together with your intent."

As naturally as breathing, and with just as much consideration, Doric reached out with one finger to touch the place between the two broken pieces. The power of growth surged in her, coming up from the soil, and she channeled it carefully into her hand. Before her eyes, the two pieces of the stake became one again, as whole as if they'd never been damaged in the first place.

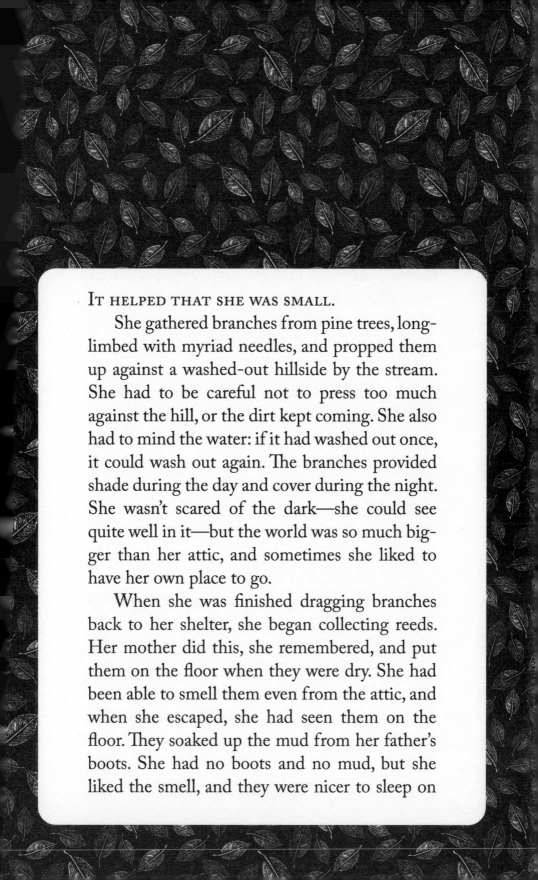

IT HELPED THAT SHE WAS SMALL.

She gathered branches from pine trees, long-limbed with myriad needles, and propped them up against a washed-out hillside by the stream. She had to be careful not to press too much against the hill, or the dirt kept coming. She also had to mind the water: if it had washed out once, it could wash out again. The branches provided shade during the day and cover during the night. She wasn't scared of the dark—she could see quite well in it—but the world was so much bigger than her attic, and sometimes she liked to have her own place to go.

When she was finished dragging branches back to her shelter, she began collecting reeds. Her mother did this, she remembered, and put them on the floor when they were dry. She had been able to smell them even from the attic, and when she escaped, she had seen them on the floor. They soaked up the mud from her father's boots. She had no boots and no mud, but she liked the smell, and they were nicer to sleep on than the ground. She had to replace them every once in a while, but she had so much else to do that it wasn't too much of an additional burden.

The main problem was clothing. She had already torn her dress to make a space for her tail, and she kept catching the hem on branches and briars, which tore it even further. The sleeves were short, so her arms were constantly cut and bruised, and she had no extra fabric to work with. She wished she'd stolen something on her abortive trip home. Or that her father had been more thoughtful when he'd abandoned her in the forest.

It occurred to her then that maybe he didn't think she would actually survive. It didn't matter what she was wearing, because she wouldn't be wearing it long. Animals and insects would take care of her body. Birds would use the shredded cloth in their nests, and that would be the end of everyone's problems. She was suddenly very determined to live.

She found berries and wrapped them in leaves before placing them out of the sun. They didn't keep long, but she discovered that it didn't matter. Even when they were spoiled, she could eat them without problems. She collected fiddleheads and bark. Not a tremendous amount, but enough that she didn't have to spend all her time looking for food to supplement what she hunted.

One day, it was sunny and bright, and the

shelter was feeling small. It was hot in the sun and boring in the shade. She saw fish jumping in the stream and thought, "Why not?" Her shoes and stockings—what was left of them—came off, followed by her bloomers. She pulled the dress over her head. Before she could give it too much thought, she plunged into the water.

It was cold, but delightfully so. She was up to her waist before she slowed down enough for her thoughts to catch up with her. Her tail floated behind her, and she relished moving it through the water. She took a deep breath and dunked herself, water running out of her hair when she stood back up. Her horns stopped itching for the first time in days.

She had cleaned herself up every day as best she could, but washing at the stream's edge and bathing in it were two different things. She found some soapwort—shuddering briefly when she remembered the trial and error that had led her to that plant in the first place—and lathered up, scrubbing down every part of her body from the tips of her horns to the tip of her tail. Her skin was pink from scrubbing when she was done, and she floated on her back for a while, wondering what the fish thought about when they were down below.

The owl came back to roost on a tree by the water. It was daylight, so the bird wasn't active, but she still felt like it was watching her. Why she would interest an owl, she had no idea.

Maybe it was as bored as she was, and it probably couldn't go swimming without ruining its feathers.

While she floated, she let her mind wander. The owl waited until she was out of the water before it glided off on the night's hunt. She shook the water out of her hair and pushed as much of it off her skin as she could before she put her dress back on. It was a little damp, but it wasn't cold, so she wasn't uncomfortable. She definitely wanted to try that again, but she would have to come up with a way to make sure that she stayed safe.

She climbed the little hill to her little shelter and crawled inside. The attic was bigger, and the food she ate there was easier to chew, but she preferred this. She knew where she was now. She knew a little bit about what the world was like. She was finding the edges, and she probably always would be, but at least out here, she was allowed to look.

CHAPTER 11

In the days that followed, they weren't needed very much in the garden. Kaliope and her assistants could tend it as its crops grew through the summer. Harvest would be another matter, but that was weeks away. Palanus still hadn't returned from whatever task they had gone off to do, and so the young druids were passed off to various other teachers in their absence. A six-foot-tall dragonborn druid named Arrhur taught them simple spells to manipulate flames and water, while his partner, Ash, helped them reach out to nature for divine guidance.

"Your power will grow as you practice what the others teach you," Ash said, spreading zher hands wide.

"And you'll build on what you've already learned with experience."

It was a sound enough theory, but Doric sometimes felt like she wouldn't possibly be able to remember everything she was learning. She didn't think she was the only one who felt that way. Leander got extra sour when he didn't master something immediately, and Gragwen could often be heard muttering to herself as she repeated back everything she'd done during the day. Jowenys was cheerful enough, but even her enthusiasm was starting to flag a little bit.

They hadn't seen Palanus since the night that Doric had arrived and been added to the training group. But when the trainees came out to breakfast the next morning, there was an eighth place set at the table, and Palanus arrived to take the last seat.

In the bright sunlight of the morning and with Open's cheerful whistling drifting in from the kitchen, Palanus looked far less mysterious than they had that first night. There was still plenty to look at, though. They were easily six and a half feet tall, and built as solidly as a brick wall; there was no mistaking a half-orc, even if they were buttering toast at the breakfast table.

"Good morning," Palanus said, reaching for the jam. "I'd eat if I were you. We have a bit of a walk ahead of us."

They scrambled into their seats and dug in. This morning Open had done something with eggs, bread, and powdered sugar that was delicious, if messy.

"Where are we going?" asked Gragwen, speaking through a mouthful of food. She must have been fairly practiced at it because it was always easy to understand what she was saying.

"We are going to find a quiet place," Palanus said. "I haven't been here for a while, and I understand that you kept busy in my absence. I would like to assess you. We will be joined by two of my friends, a ranger and a barbarian. The druid outlook is not the only one, and it's important that you do not focus so closely on your studies that you forget everything else."

They gave the distinct impression of not wanting to answer any more questions, and so Doric and the others ate their breakfast without asking any, even though they each had several. Open came in with some pinecone syrup to pour on the bread. It was so sweet that it made Doric's teeth ache, but Mistral poured so much onto his plate that his breakfast was in danger of floating away.

Finally, Palanus finished their breakfast and polished their tusks with a napkin.

"Thank you, Open," they said. "As for the rest of you, follow me."

Palanus had a long stride, and keeping up with them did not allow for much in the way of conversation. After a few minutes, Jowenys hoisted Gragwen onto her shoulders, because the halfling was hard-pressed to keep up. They followed Palanus deeper into the forest than any of them had yet been, farther from the camp and farther into the trees. Here, the woods were even wilder. There were vines wrapped around tree trunks, and the scent of pine needles was heavy in the air. The branches of cedar trees brushed against them as they walked, and they scanned the ground for rocks so they didn't trip. It was gradual at first, but before long it became apparent that they were heading uphill.

After about half an hour, they burst into a sunlit glade. There was a rock wall at the back of it, and cascading down from above was a crystal-clear waterfall. The water fell into a small grotto, which must have been a lot deeper than it looked, because there was no stream or creek running out of it. The grotto was ringed by ice-white boulders flecked with gray spots, and elegant trees provided some shade near the water.

"Take a seat," Palanus intoned, and each of them scrambled up onto a boulder.

It wasn't the most comfortable seat, but Doric had to admit that the view from her vantage point was beautiful. She could see down into the grotto, which was indeed the mouth of a cave. The water that fell into it would disappear into an aquafer, filtering through stone for centuries until it returned to the surface somewhere else in the cave system. Doric closed her eyes as the others settled in and let the warmth of the sun and the music of the falling water match the rhythm of her breathing.

"Leander, if you would," Palanus said, pointing to the water.

It was clear that Leander didn't understand what he was being asked to do at first, but after a slightly awkward moment, he sat up straight and held his hands out towards the water. With the now familiar sounds and gestures, he raised a bit of water from the surface, stretching it into a rope that was several feet long. When he let it go, it splashed back into the grotto. Doric and

Jowenys exchanged a look. Leander had been able to make far more elaborate shapes than that. It didn't make sense that he couldn't do it now.

"Doric," Palanus said.

Doric took a deep breath and tried the cantrip. Even though Arrhur had been guiding her through it for a few days, she struggled to lift the water just as Leander had. Her shape was a flat disk, which created a much bigger splash when it fell back into the grotto, but Doric knew her performance hadn't been any better than Leander's.

One by one, each of them tried to call and manipulate the water as they had been learning, and one by one, they struggled. Remigold was the most frustrated by his failure. He always put a lot of pressure on himself and took perceived shortcomings to heart.

"You have all done better than I expected," Palanus said. "Have any of you guessed why it's so much harder for you out here?"

Doric thought about it. In the garden, Kaliope had put things in her hands and whispered the words she would need. When Arrhur taught them about fire, he was always monitoring them closely to make sure the flames didn't go awry.

"It's because we're doing it by ourselves." Mistral spoke up just before Doric could. "It's harder because we're working without a guide. When the others taught us, they sort of pushed us in the right direction. We learned it, but we didn't learn how to generate it entirely from within."

"That is correct," Palanus said. "And it is not a flaw

in your learning or their teaching. Rather, it is the nature of magic. The waterfall has been digging out this grotto for a very, very long time, yet for the drops that fall in now to reach the bottom, they must find the right direction in the churning of the pool. That is what you must do."

Palanus had them continue to practice as the sun rose higher and higher overhead. It was the longest time any of them had spent continuously practicing magic, yet the more Doric cast, the more confident she felt in the result. It was like her brain and body were allowing the druidic magic to settle in, walking a path she'd traversed enough times that she no longer needed to look where she was going. They shaped water and fire and earth. They practiced making flowers bud. Gragwen conjured the smell of a skunk, which sent them all fleeing out of her range but also made them laugh.

When Palanus finally called a halt, they were all very pleased with themselves. Remigold was still chattering about how much they had improved when two strangers entered the clearing. Palanus didn't seem surprised, and when the two figures came closer, Doric recognized them as the dwarf ranger and the half-elf barbarian she had seen with Palanus before.

"This is Elessa," Palanus said, indicating the barbarian. "And this is Bramdain. They are going to take you on a short camping trip before you come back to the Enclave."

"But we don't have any gear," Leander protested.

"Yes." Bramdain nodded. "And you barely know any magic, from what I've heard."

"Don't be cruel," Elessa rebuked him. "They are doing their best."

"Druids must be self-sufficient," Palanus said. "You all have basic survival skills from before you arrived, and you have all been learning about how to function as a group from Kaliope. It is time to remember how to survive on your own."

"With a few friends," Bramdain said. "We're coming with you."

"I will see you in a couple of days," Palanus said. They stood up from their boulder, stretched out a kink in their neck from sitting all day, and set off in the direction of the Enclave encampment.

"You know, I am not sure about their teaching methods," Cassa said.

"We're learning, aren't we?" said Jowenys.

"We don't have time to talk about it." Doric brought them back to reality. "If we're camping somewhere else for the night, we're going to have to move soon. The sun is high, but it gets dark quickly in the forest, and then it'll be hard for some of you to navigate."

"The redheaded girl is right," Elessa said. "Follow Bramdain, and he can take you to our first stop."

It was easy following a dwarf through the forest, even one who was an expert ranger and moved pretty quickly. Gragwen kept up on her own as well as any of them. They walked away from the grotto, heading into the dimmer light of the forest again. Bramdain didn't take them very far, but Doric noticed that they had started walking downhill again by the time they stopped.

"First step," said Bramdain. "Build a shelter."

For a moment, the young druids stood looking at one another, and then Doric sighed. She didn't enjoy being in charge of things. It was always easier to pass that sort of thing to Torrieth, who was more suited to being the center of attention. But it was clear that, of all of them, she was the one with the most experience. She just had to be careful that she used only the knowledge she'd learned from Fenjor and didn't stir up any unwelcome memories about the first time she'd used her survival skills on her own.

"You'll want to find branches," she said. "Long ones, as many as possible, still with their needles on them. Then we'll need to find something to lean them up against. That's the easiest way to build a small shelter quickly."

"What about everything else?" Leander asked accusingly. "We're going to need something for dinner and a firepit. We can't all just run off looking for branches."

It galled her a little bit, but he was right.

"Leander, you take Remigold and Jowenys to look for branches for the shelter," Doric directed. "We haven't been walking downhill very long, so, Cassa and Mistral, I want you to go back up and see if you can find us a place to build a few lean-tos. Gragwen, you're on foraging duty."

"What about you?" Leander demanded.

"I'm going to find water," Doric said. "That waterfall had to come from somewhere, and as I said, we haven't been walking downhill very long. Hopefully by the time

I locate it, we'll have a campsite, and then we can dig the firepit and the latrine."

The others scattered to go about their various tasks. Bramdain and Elessa watched without providing guidance, which Doric took as approval, or at least as an indication that none of them were going to die. Doric tried to remember the path they'd taken to get here and whether she'd seen any signs of water that they had just walked past.

"Well done," Elessa said, surveying their progress a few hours later. "It's always easier to work with nature than against it. That goes for the wilds, and for the natures of the people you're with."

"I'll be more impressed if it actually works," Bramdain said. Then he grinned. "But it's a good start."

"It was," Doric thought. The lean-tos would be drafty, and they would have to go get more firewood before they turned in for the night, but the camp had come together pretty well. Even latrine-digging duty hadn't been too onerous. Gragwen came back with pockets full of mushrooms and then disappeared again, saying something about some leaf they could eat along with them. One by one, the others finished their tasks and came to gather around the firepit. Between the lesson, the hike, and the setup, they were tired, but Doric could tell they were proud of themselves, too.

Moreover, she had taken initiative, and it had been a good thing. She hadn't thought it was in her nature to lead, but maybe that was just something else she'd learn how to take control of while she was learning to become a druid.

CHAPTER 12

"Have any of you ever fought anything before?" Palanus asked as they ate breakfast several days later. They'd arrived home from their impromptu camping trip the previous night after a few days of roughing it in the woods, mostly hale and healthy, though very much in need of baths and, in Leander's case, a remedy for poison oak. They were all attacking Open's hot breakfast with considerable gusto.

"I used to push my brother in the creek," Gragwen said. "Does that count?"

"Did he fight back?" Palanus asked.

"Well, yes," Gragwen said. "And he did try to dump me first."

"Then it counts," Palanus declared. "Anyone else?"

There was no answer. Doric wasn't really surprised, though she was a bit curious as to why Leander hadn't also admitted to scrummaging with his siblings. He always wanted to look more experienced. Maybe he was an only child.

Palanus finished eating and neatly wiped the corner of their mouth before polishing each tusk.

"When you're finished, come out to the clearing," Palanus told them. "Don't take too long."

They were less than two minutes behind Palanus. No one wanted to fight on a full stomach anyway.

Palanus took them to the far end of the clearing, to the area where the rangers had set up their targets. These had been pushed out of the way this morning, opening the dewy grass for whatever Palanus had in mind. After the camping trip, Doric felt like anything might happen, but at least they were still within sight of where they slept. She could handle anything here. Probably. The idea of combat made her a bit nervous. She hunted, and she argued, but the thought of turning the spells she'd learned to fighting was altogether different.

"Druids do not fight for good, and they do not fight for evil," Palanus said. "We fight for balance, for nature. Today we will practice what you already know."

Around the half-orc, the wind picked up. It didn't escape farther than six feet in a circle around them, which meant they held it perfectly under control. Doric felt herself shifting away from them instinctively, not knowing where the strike would come from or what it would be. There was nothing to hide behind here, and nothing she could see that could be called for defense. They hadn't even stopped to get armor and shields on their way out. Her sling was in the pocket on her belt because she hadn't clipped it to her arm yet, and she had only a few stones in that same pocket.

The earth rumbled around Palanus's feet, the effect rippling out around them, as though they were the epicenter of an earthquake. Jowenys and Cassa tried to jump to avoid the shaking, but the ground they landed on was still moving, and they didn't stay standing. Remigold and Gragwen tried to stay on their feet and were unsuccessful. Mistral at least fell gracefully. Doric dexterously maneuvered over the unstable ground until she escaped the range of the tremors. She was aware that Leander had done the same thing, and they were the only two still on their feet when the ground stilled.

"Well, I've seen worse," Palanus said thoughtfully. "At least you all tried to do something. But why wasn't that something a spell?"

Doric blinked. Even Jowenys didn't have a quick answer, and she usually had an answer for everything.

"Druids fight defensively for the most part," Palanus said. "We find weakness, we surprise, we make the very ground untrustworthy. It seems to go against nature, but the truth is that nature is holding back a great deal of the time. When you fight, try the spells that come the most easily to you, and practice using them in creative ways."

They tried their best to dodge while Palanus firmly recited an incantation. Plants grew out of nowhere to ensnare their feet, and they all danced free. Only Mistral had the presence of mind to try burning them, with limited success. A violent downdraft of wind threatened to knock them all on their backsides again, but Doric was able to push back against the wind with a gust of her own and keep her feet. When Jowenys and Remigold came and stood beside her, it got easier as they pushed together.

"Those are the basics," Palanus said. "We'll get to the others later when we're all somewhere less breakable. For now, please pair up. I'd like you to try sparring by way of spellcasting. Carefully."

Palanus directed Remigold to be their partner, causing the elf to turn a little pale. He took off his hat and went to face his fate. The others arranged themselves, and Doric found herself opposite Leander. Jowenys caught her eye and shrugged as if to say "someone has to, and it's your turn."

"All right," Leander taunted. "What have you got?"

Doric pulled power up from the earth and into her body and sent a bank of fog in his direction. It was a bit bigger than she intended, sweeping up Gragwen as well. The halfling didn't seem to mind and used it to her advantage in her own duel with Mistral. A swift wind came forth from Leander, dissipating the fog. Doric moved quickly to avoid getting caught in the gust, rolling on the ground to his left. Before the fog had entirely cleared, Leander pressed the attack, lashing a whip made of thorns right at her. Doric raised her hands defensively and made her skin rough and hard like tree bark. The whip glanced off her with no effect. She was already starting to breathe heavily, and she saw that he was flagging as well. His hands stretched out in front of his chest just before she made the same movement, only nothing happened. Doric dug deep to the last bits of her strength and channeled a wave of force directly at Leander, sending him flying back. She immediately sank to her knees, sweating and panting.

"Do you want to know what you did wrong?" Palanus asked conversationally.

Doric realized that the other fights had already stopped, too. Remigold was still standing. Jowenys had jumped across the arena, and the others were all in various states of disarray.

"Spells take up your energy," Palanus said. "The more you use, the more exhausted you become. That's why Leander conjured up nothing towards the end of his skirmish. I'm actually somewhat impressed by how long you all lasted. Someone must have really drummed the theory into your heads while I was away."

"So what's the point of combat?" Leander demanded, red-faced from exertion and embarrassment. "If we can only do a few things, we might as well not fight at all."

"First of all, if you're lucky, you won't be fighting alone," Palanus said. "Second, the point of practicing is to get stronger. If you hadn't spent two weeks working already, you'd all be flat out, not standing around grumbling at me. You will get better, and when you're like me, you can do a whole host of things without straining."

"Does that mean we're done for the day?" Mistral asked.

"Of course not," Palanus said. "I'm going to teach you mundane ways of fighting, too, for backup. Doric, are you any good with that sling, or do you just carry it around for sentimental purposes?"

Doric clipped the sling to her arm and looked around for some suitable stones. Near the edge of the clearing, a few had been shaken loose by the earthquake. They weren't perfect, but they'd do for now.

"What do you want me to hit?" she asked.

Palanus directed them to an outdoor rack of training weapons. Jowenys and Leander practiced staff forms. Cassa had a crossbow. The others took up bows and arrows and lined up alongside Doric. Palanus made targets out of clumps of dirt, which was fun because that meant they kind of exploded when you hit them. By the time dinner rolled around, Jowenys and Leander had bruised knuckles, Cassa had shown Remigold how to use the crossbow, and Mistral had improved enough that he could explode one of the dirt clumps in two shots.

"Not bad for your first day," Palanus said. "We'll try something more exciting tomorrow."

Doric was a little worried about what that might be, but then she imagined standing on a hilltop calling lightning down, or turning into a giant bug to scare off some humans, and decided it would definitely be worth it.

SEVERAL WEEKS LATER, Open came with them to combat practice. He didn't say why, but all of them were a little excited. The tiefling was clearly strong, and he couldn't spend all his time cooking. He joined Palanus in the center of the training area.

"Today Open and I are going to show you the basics of Wild Shape," Palanus announced. "Like many druid talents, this one will improve as your power increases. You'll be able to change into bigger animals, hold the shape for longer, and even fly in the right form with time."

An excited murmur swept through the young druids. Doric clenched her fists with anticipation. Wild Shape had intrigued her since she had first heard of it. She understood that all druidic skills had to be studied and practiced deliberately for them to become second nature, but she was more excited about this particular lesson than any other.

Palanus demonstrated first, showing how they shifted from their own form into that of a huge white wolf. Open went next. His technique was a bit different, but it still worked, and soon enough a dappled horse stood next to the wolf. They changed back and forth a few times, repeating the demonstration with smaller animals that would be easier to change into, and then it was time.

Despite their best efforts and dogged determination, it took hours of concentration and frustration before Leander finally managed to change into a rabbit. He barely managed to hop before he retook his own form, but he was grinning widely when he was human again. Doric couldn't even be annoyed that he had been successful first, because something about his transformation locked the spell together in her mind. Before he could start bragging about it, she turned into a fox.

Doric wasn't able to hold the shape any longer than Leander had, but she was elated nonetheless. Open clapped her on the shoulder as congratulations, and the others looked only mildly jealous. Palanus had them practice for a little while longer, but by the end of the session, only Leander and Doric had managed the change at all, and neither of them had been able to hold it.

"It will come with time," Palanus promised. It didn't seem reassuring to the others.

Since she had been successful, Doric volunteered to draw water from the nearby stream for the evening's cooking. Leander also volunteered, but only after Open raised his eyebrows at him, and with extreme reluctance. The others went off to soothe their pride and relax while Doric and Leander took the buckets and set out.

"I noticed that you only learned how to Wild Shape when you saw me do it," Leander said as they trudged back with their heavy loads.

"That's how it works," Doric said. "We saw Open and Palanus do it, too."

"Yeah, but you only learn when someone hands it right to you," Leander said. "And don't think I'm the only one who has noticed."

"What are you talking about?" Doric asked. Her temper was rising fast.

"I've heard what you talk about with Jowenys," Leander sneered. "The wood elves only accepted you because of your guardian. She handed you a home and a best friend. You weren't good at being a ranger, so she told you that maybe you should be a druid instead."

Doric stopped walking and set the bucket down. Hearing these words from Leander was like scratching at an open wound with a knife. He'd been eavesdropping on her this whole time, and now he was preying on her weak spots, just like Palanus said a druid should do.

"Then you came here," Leander continued. "And maybe you can set up a campsite, but you never make magical progress until someone else does. You've never done anything for yourself, unlike the rest of us. As soon as your so-called family back home realizes that you're a leech, they'll make sure you stay away."

Doric's temper snapped. She hurled the water bucket at him, but he dodged easily.

"Are you done with your tantrum?" Leander asked. He sounded spiteful, and so much in control that she wanted to tear his skin off.

"No," Doric said. She straightened but didn't relax her stance. "What you said was completely uncalled for, and you're *wrong*."

Leander scowled, annoyed that she had stood up for herself. Now he was like a bear with a sore paw. But Doric had faced a bear before, and she wasn't scared. He shifted his weight, and Doric prepared for any kind of defense, but he chose a different route of attack first.

"Was it so uncalled for? Or just truth you didn't want to hear?" he asked. "You were raised by wood elves who only care about you because you might be useful to them, and that usefulness you didn't even earn. You don't belong anywhere."

Doric wanted to scream at him. Every doubt that had haunted her dreams since she was a child, and everything she had fought to overcome after, dug into her brain. She knew that Liavaris and Torrieth cared about her and wanted her to come back. If the others found her likeable because she was useful, then that was enough. Even though she'd thought she was a solitary person, she hadn't liked being alone on her journey here. She couldn't imagine disappearing into a forest somewhere for the rest of her life with only spirits and the occasional courageous chipmunk for company. But the nagging feeling that had followed her since childhood flared up at his words.

Doric felt the strength of the mountain surge beneath her feet, the wind and the trees and the raw force of everything around her unlocking a new depth of power. She could have blasted him to pieces, she felt, but at the last minute she changed her mind. There was something even better, a way to beat him that would hurt him even more. Like Palanus said, a clever druid can win by thinking creatively.

She was beyond rational thought, watching as he fell into a defensive posture waiting for her to strike. She felt wild, like a fire burning out of control. The grin she gave him was feral, but she didn't notice when he shrank away. She threw her head back and roared.

Then she Wild Shaped into a bear.

EVEN THE NEVERWINTER WOOD COULD BE wracked by storms. The weather was strange and warm, but above and beyond the forest, normal skies brought rain and snow in accordance with the seasons. A deluge would fall in the north of the forest, and the southern creeks would swell days later in response. It was the way of things in the woods—as ferocious as the world outside, but fierce in different ways.

She kept an eye on the sky, waiting for the storms to come. When she lived in the attic, sometimes clouds would block her window and rain would fall. Other times, the window would be laced with frost and snow would cover the ground. That did not happen here, and after a time, she stopped being quite so watchful.

The first sign was that the forest grew quiet.

The bird calls ceased, and even the insects were still. It was as if everything were holding its breath, waiting for something to happen. She stuck her head out of the shelter, trying to see what was wrong. The forest animals usually gave some sort of signal if there was danger, like a predator or an angry wild boar, but now they, too, were silent.

She crawled out of the shelter and stood up. She was still so small, though she burst at the seams of her clothes. When the flood came, it swept her away as easily as if she were a dry pine branch leaning against a washed-out hill.

Her first instinct was to kick. She flailed wildly, trying to keep her head above the rushing water. She had taught herself a little bit of swimming, but this wasn't a simple float or bath in the friendly and familiar creek. This was a raging torrent that pulled her inexorably on, and fighting it sapped her energy much faster than she expected. Before long, even keeping her head above water was almost more than she could handle.

A flash of white caught her eye, and she tried to look up into the bright blue sky. The leaves on the trees made it hard to focus, splitting light around them, and the water demanded her attention, but soon enough she locked eyes on something familiar. The owl was above her, gliding on peaceful wings that belied the frothy waters in which she struggled. It couldn't help her. Even if the water were calm, its wings were too soft and would quickly become waterlogged. In the face of the rushing flood, the owl could only watch and wait.

She knew she didn't have much time. Each breath was a struggle; each fight to break the surface was one step closer to being her last. She felt the rage of the water all around her, but she couldn't focus enough to do anything like she had when she watched the owl hunt. Her mind was in a panic, unable to draw on memory or any instinct beyond the fight to breathe. She watched the owl fly away and wanted to scream, but she knew that if she did, it would only hasten her end.

She swallowed water, gasping and spitting and only taking in more. She kicked and kicked and kicked, her shoes long gone and her skirt dragging her down. She hadn't looked out the attic window for this. She hadn't found her way home and then turned away for this. She hadn't eked out a living in the forest all this time on her own for this. She was made for something more, she was sure of it, and she wasn't going to let the flood take her from it.

With one last burst of strength, she kicked for the shore. She tried to use the current, angling herself so that it pulled her along, but it was almost impossible. She didn't have the endurance to hold out much longer. And still she kicked, casting about for the bottom when she thought she might be able to touch it.

Finally, just as the last of her spirit gave up, her hands closed on a rock and her feet hit the bottom. Her knees scraped along the stones, and she didn't care. She heaved herself towards solid ground, shredding her skin as she went, until she collapsed on the bank. She gasped for air, spitting up the last of the water before flopping onto her back in relief.

A shadow blocked the light. It was a woman with white hair and pointed ears. An elf, then.

"Breathe easy, child," a voice said. It was so kind and so warm she was sure she imagined it. "We are going to take you home."

CHAPTER 13

Doric had always thought that rage and the bear went hand in hand. Standing on her hind legs and roaring, she felt the power of it sweep through her. She wasn't surprised that her massive new shape was capable of so much anger. She had seen it before as the bear rampaged through the destructive logging site. What she hadn't been prepared for was the absolute clarity in her own mind when she was in the bear's skin. The anger didn't belong to the bear. It belonged to her.

She looked down at Leander, who had thrown his bucket down and was running back towards the clearing as fast as he could. She dropped to all fours and ambled after him. She wasn't really interested in mauling him, though she had to admit that scaring him was somewhat satisfying. He had made her feel awful, and it was nice to see all that smug superiority fall right off his face when he was faced with something he knew he couldn't match.

Doric broke through the edge of the clearing just behind Leander. He was still running full tilt and breezed past Jowenys without a second look at her. Jowenys started to yell at him but then heard the unmistakable noise of a large animal coming close and turned around. She looked up at Doric-the-bear, and absolute terror flashed across her face.

Doric pulled back so quickly she would have tripped had she not been standing on four legs. She immediately dropped to her haunches, lowering her body to the ground to appear as unthreatening as possible. Scaring Leander was one thing. She didn't want anyone else to be scared of her.

"Doric?" There was a tremulous note in Jowenys's voice that Doric had never heard before, but all she could do was nod. "Don't move. I'll be right back."

Jowenys fled into the cabin, and the full weight of what she had done slammed into Doric's chest. She buried her face in her paws with an animal groan. All of her plans to be useful and learn control, and this was what she did? She wanted to grow her talents, to be reliable. Safe. She didn't want people to be afraid of her. That was the entire point of her studies with the Emerald Enclave, and yet here she was, scaring the person who had been the very first to accept her. She tried to change back into her own shape, but she was so upset she couldn't do it.

"Doric!" Palanus emerged from the cabin, calling her name. A few of the other Enclave members had started drifting towards them, too, even more people to witness her shame.

"Let me," Open said from behind them. Palanus nodded and moved aside.

Open walked towards her slowly, and Doric stayed on the ground. She didn't want someone understanding and gentle to be the one to throw her out. She wanted it to be someone she didn't care about, someone whose opinion of her didn't matter as much.

"Are you stuck?" Open asked.

Doric nodded miserably.

"All right, then," Open said. He took off the apron he was wearing and set it on the grass. Then he closed his eyes for a moment and changed into a bear.

He walked towards the forest, turning to look at Doric when she didn't follow him. He cocked his head in a way that could only mean "you coming?" regardless of what species he was, and Doric hauled herself to her feet. She shuffled after him into the trees, her head low, trusting him to lead, because she couldn't stand the thought of looking up.

Open led her only a short way into the forest before he stopped and turned around. Doric wanted to slump back onto the ground but remained on her feet. She knew she would tire eventually and the change would reverse itself on its own, but she was sad she would begin her exile as a bear. She couldn't talk, so she couldn't thank the Enclave for trying, couldn't tell them that knowing them had almost made her a better person.

When Open was sure she was looking, he shifted back into his own shape. He took a few steps towards her and then reached out a hand to scratch her shoulder. It was almost more than Doric could take, but she didn't flinch away from him. He had been so kind to her. She owed him some dignity before she left.

"You have to want to be yourself again," Open said.

If Doric had been her own shape, she might have cried. At least a bear was expected to live alone in the forest. Doric had sometimes thought that living by herself would solve a lot of her problems, but she knew that wasn't who she was. She *had* lived alone, and it had been awful. She didn't want to do it again. But the idea of spending the rest of her life as someone who was always suspicious, always just a little bit feared, was just as bad. And now she knew that people had a reason to be afraid of her. She had *enjoyed* scaring Leander. She had been proud of herself.

"Doric, sometimes this just happens," Open said. "Do you think everyone liked me when I arrived here? Do you think Palanus was immediately embraced as a leader? Even Kaliope has her moments, and she looks like everyone's grandmother until you remember what she can do with a root system. People fear things. That's just who we are."

Doric sighed, a great, silly noise from a bear, but she didn't care anymore. She concentrated on her regular shape, wanting it as much as she could, and a few moments later, she stood on her own two feet.

"There," Open consoled. "That's much better."

He sat down on a log, holding his tail in one hand until he was settled and then draping it behind him. Doric came and sat beside him, ready to face her fate.

"Your change was impressive, I will admit," Open said. That wasn't what Doric was expecting. "You held it for a long time, and it's a big animal. Palanus told me that you and Leander had both managed smaller creatures, so this is a great improvement. You should be proud of your progress."

"But I misused it," Doric said.

"Yes." Open tilted his head knowingly. "You did. And I'm sure Leander was completely blameless in the whole situation."

Doric wouldn't rat him out, mostly because she didn't want to tell anyone what he had said. She just stared wordlessly at her fists resting tensely on her legs.

"Look," Open continued. "I am supposed to take you to task for using your power against an ally, but I think you're doing a fine job of it yourself, eh? So I'll just tell you not to do it again, and I know you won't, because you do legitimately feel bad about it."

"I mostly feel bad for scaring Jowenys," Doric admitted.

"You can apologize to her when you get back," Open

said. "You'll probably have to apologize to both of them, but I know she's your friend, so she means more to you."

"When I get back?" Doric asked quietly. She was still looking down, afraid of what she would see in Open's face.

"We're not going to make you leave, Doric," Open said.

Doric scuffed her boot in the dirt and finally looked up.

"You said some people didn't like you when you got here," she blurted out before she could change her mind. "How did you change that? What did you do?"

Open laughed, leaning back precariously on the log, but it wasn't a mean sound. Rather, it sounded like he was free. It was one of the most beautiful things Doric had ever heard.

"You can't change people," he said. "I mean, you can change them a bit, but some people are always going to be small-minded. You can change yourself, but you have to decide if those people are worth it. If you decide that they're not, you go and find other people."

"What if you never find the right people?" she asked.

"Doric," Open said. "You've already started."

He got to his feet and held out a hand to help her up. She didn't need it, but she took it anyway.

"Maybe keep the Wild Shaping in the training area for now, though," he said. There was a smile in his voice, which lessened her anxiety, and she gave a nervous bark of laughter of her own.

"Definitely," she agreed. "I want to make sure I can control it completely before I try it again."

"That's the spirit," Open said. "Now let's go home

before Palanus manages to completely incinerate the pheasants I am roasting for dinner."

Doric followed him back to the clearing. She still had a lot of work to do, but at least she knew where she would be while she did it.

CHAPTER 14

Palanus had not burned the pheasants, but Doric barely tasted them. Gragwen had welcomed her to the table with a small smile, and Mistral had immediately started asking questions about what it was like to be a bear. Remigold shushed him, which gave Doric enough time to steel herself for the task ahead. First she turned to Leander.

"I'm sorry, Leander," she said. "I shouldn't have reacted the way I did, and I shouldn't have used my powers against you."

Leander clearly wanted to say something biting, but Jowenys and Gragwen were both glaring daggers at him. He only drew himself up and muttered, "Apology accepted."

"Jowenys, I never wanted to scare you." Doric swallowed around the lump in her throat. She didn't care if Leander forgave her, but she was hoping Jowenys would. "I'm so sorry."

"I knew it was you," Jowenys said. "And I knew that druids stay themselves, no matter their shape. You just startled me. You're a very big bear."

Doric wasn't entirely sure that was the truth, but if Jowenys was willing to accept her, then Doric was willing to take her at her word.

"Now will you *please* tell us what it was like?" Mistral said, mouth full of pheasant.

Doric started to cut up her meat and explained as best she could. Leander was sulking, and Palanus still hadn't said anything to her, but her fellow students seemed to forgive her, or at least be interested enough in how she did it to let any bad feelings go. Palanus just watched while she ate and talked, distracting her from both.

"Do you feel taller?" Remigold asked.

"She was taller," Jowenys said. "At least on her hind legs."

"It's hard to describe. I know it's not helpful, but you'll understand when you do it." Doric looked tentatively at Leander and decided to extend an olive branch. "Right, Leander? No matter what creature you become."

Leander stabbed his fork into the meat on his plate and didn't answer. Doric felt a bit deflated and was glad when Jowenys changed the subject. As much as she disliked him, Leander had as much right to be here as she did. She didn't want him to think that she was getting special treatment. He probably thought she deserved to be punished. Doric didn't speak for the rest of the meal, eating mechanically without being aware of what she was chewing. As they stood up to leave, Palanus finally turned their attention to her and indicated that she should remain at the table. Leander smirked.

"I know that Open has already told you how inappropriate your behavior was, so I won't dwell on it," Palanus said. Any good feeling Doric had managed to claw her way back to dissipated fast. "I will merely remind you that the Emerald Enclave works towards common purpose, no matter who or what the members are. Even if we don't get along perfectly with all of them, it's important that we learn to work with everyone."

"I understand," Doric said. "My whole purpose in coming here was to learn to control my powers and be helpful to others, and today I failed. I won't fail again."

"Open tells me you plan to reserve your Wild Shape for training," Palanus continued. "I think that is a good idea for the foreseeable future."

Doric nodded. It was hard to tell if they were disappointed in her or if they were just doing their job as her teacher, but it didn't really matter. At this point, both were the same thing.

"You may go," Palanus said. Doric stood up and started walking towards the door. "Oh, and Doric?"

"Yes?" She paused.

"Should you need it, there are several senior druids, myself included, who can Wild Shape into bears," Palanus said. "Your training doesn't have to stall out while you wait for the others to catch up. We will be cautious: control is important. You can learn just as much control by being a bear as you can by not being a bear."

Doric wasn't entirely sure she believed them. She knew Jowenys was putting on a brave face, but Doric never wanted anyone to look at her the way her friend had ever again. In a way, her trust was an even bigger burden than Torrieth's was. Torrieth trusted her because they had grown up together, and because she thought she knew what Doric was capable of. Jowenys actually knew what Doric was capable of, and how to fight her if it came to that. Doric couldn't break her trust again.

She was still deep in her thoughts when she got back to the room she shared with Jowenys. The firbolg was sitting on Doric's bunk, a melted candle and some uncarded wool in her hands.

"I found the crack in the wall where Leander was eavesdropping on us," she said by way of explanation. "I'm blocking it up as best I can."

Doric made a disbelieving noise. She did not deserve this girl.

"How did you know he was eavesdropping?" she asked.

"Well, I figured there were a lot of reasons he could have made you mad enough to Wild Shape," Jowenys said. "But he made you mad enough that you turned into a bear, so I thought he must have said something dreadful. The only way he could know what dreadful thing to say was if he heard us talking, so I went looking for weak spots in the timber, and here we are."

Only a few hours ago, Doric thought she was going to have to leave. Not only was she staying, but Jowenys had also made their room safer for her and her secrets.

"Thank you," she said. She sat down on the mattress beside her. "And I really am sorry that I startled you."

Jowenys giggled at her word choice and then leaned back to stuff a clump of wax and wool into a pine knot.

"My mother said it's good for your constitution," Jowenys said. "Keeps your insides moving around."

"That's . . . alarming," Doric said.

"That's why I'm sitting on your bed!" Jowenys said brightly. She pulled her hand back from the pine knot, and Doric saw that it was effectively blocked. "I think that's the last of them, but we can look again tomorrow if you want."

She got up to wash her hands in the basin.

"Palanus wasn't too angry, were they?" she asked as she cleaned up.

"No," Doric said. "They and Open just reminded me what the Emerald Enclave is about, and I agreed that I would only Wild Shape while supervised for now."

"That seems fair," Jowenys said. "I'd like to tear the hide off of Leander for hurting your feelings so badly, but I guess I'll just have to be satisfied with you scaring the pants off him."

Doric couldn't share in Jowenys's glee, but she could understand it. She had felt it, too, before she'd tamped it down and gotten her temper back under control. As she watched Jowenys putter around the room, cleaning up the mess she'd made reinforcing the wall, Doric realized that her friend had never asked her exactly what Lean-

der had said. She'd told Jowenys the basics of her childhood as they chatted in the downtime or while they
were falling asleep, but she hadn't given that many spe-
cifics. Leander must have overheard and then guessed at
her true weakness. He was certainly clever enough.

Doric felt her temper rising again but firmly shoved
it back down. No one would fear her again. Maybe
Open was brave enough to keep finding new groups of
people until he found one that accepted him as he was,
but Doric didn't feel the same way. She liked the people
she already had, and she was going to fight to keep
them, even if the person she was fighting was herself.

The decision made, Doric got up to prepare for bed,
and that was when the alarm bells started ringing.

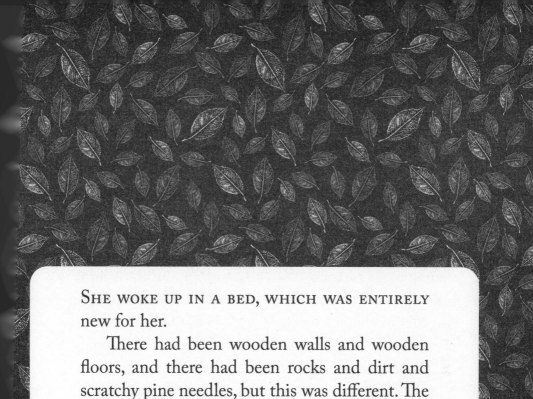

SHE WOKE UP IN A BED, WHICH WAS ENTIRELY new for her.

There had been wooden walls and wooden floors, and there had been rocks and dirt and scratchy pine needles, but this was different. The room had a clean leather smell, and there was hearthsmoke in the air. It was warm and it was dry, and there was plenty of space to breathe. She had slept beneath furs that tickled her nose. There was no scratchy straw anywhere near her. She sneezed before she remembered to stay quiet.

"Good morning," said a voice from beside her.

She froze, but whoever was close by clearly knew she was awake, so she reluctantly opened both eyes fully and blinked.

The room was bigger than she'd expected. It was simple, wooden, and with a roof high enough that her father could have stood up in the middle of it. There were cozy places to sleep and decorative trinkets adorning a few shelves. She was lying in a bed across from the door. There was a small brazier inside, just smoldering. There was also daylight, since the door of the hut was open. It was clear enough that she had to give her eyes a moment to adjust, but then she saw who was speaking to her.

A wood elf was crouched next to her, holding a bowl of water and looking at her expectantly. She was old, older than the girl's mother at any rate, and she had white hair. Her face was kind, or at least what the girl always imagined kind looked like. She didn't have any personal experience beyond knowledge of the word.

"Good morning," the girl said before the moment could drag on for too long.

"Are you lost?" the elf asked.

It was a good question, and the girl honestly wasn't sure. If she was lost, then she had been lost deliberately, and that didn't seem to be what the elf wanted to know.

"No," she said. "My father left me in the woods. I built a shelter, but there was a flood."

"How clever you are, to take care of yourself in the forest," the elf said. There was a tightness to her eyes that belied her kind words. She was furious, and she was furious because a child had been left alone.

"I built a shelter by a stream," she said. "It broke."

"Ah, but that's because the river cheated," the elf said. "If you want to stay with me, I will teach you how the river works, and it will not cheat you again. You will have a home, and you won't have to be by yourself anymore."

The girl considered the offer. No one had ever wanted her to stay before, and no one had ever offered to teach her anything either. No one usually *spoke* to her, so frankly this whole discussion was a novelty. She wasn't entirely sure how she felt about it. But the bed was comfortable, and the hut was warm.

"All right," she said. She could always run away if it didn't work out, but she had a strangely good feeling about this woman. The elf was kind. She could learn to deal with kindness.

"My name is Liavaris," the elf said. "There are many elves here. You don't have to meet them all at once, but some of them are curious about the child that was pulled from the river."

The girl said nothing for a long moment. She knew what had happened when her baby sister saw her, and what her parents had done after.

"Won't they be afraid of me?" she asked.

"Bah, if they are, then they deserve it," Liavaris said. "You are just a child, and fearing you is pointless. Later you might become something to fear if you want, but you don't have to."

"My mother was afraid," the girl said.

"Then your mother was an idiot," Liavaris said. Her tone had been light and breezy, but now she spoke seriously.

This was the longest conversation the girl

had ever had, and it was full of so many new ideas she thought her brain might burst.

"All right," the girl said. "I'll stay." And then, because she had heard it before, she added, "Thank you."

"You still look exhausted, child," Liavaris said. "Drink this, and then go back to sleep. There is nothing so important that you need to do it now, and it's better if you heal before you meet anyone else."

The girl drank the water in the bowl and then handed it back. She lay back down, glad she didn't have to get up yet. Even drinking a little bit had made her tired. She couldn't walk away if anyone made her go.

"Oh, how rude of me. I forgot," Liavaris said. "What is your name?"

"Doric," the girl said. "Or, at least, that's what my parents said when they talked about me."

Liavaris looked at her and then stroked her cheek. Doric was so surprised she almost flinched but managed not to. It was wonderful. She'd watched her mother touch the baby like this and always wondered what it was like. Now she knew. She leaned into the touch without meaning to, and Liavaris didn't take her hand away until Doric relaxed back onto her pillow.

Doric watched as a series of emotions flared across Liavaris's face. She didn't understand them, but she remembered them perfectly afterward. As the years went on, she would come to identify them: fury, pity, and a tenderness so vast that she always shied away from it. The important thing now was that none of them were fear. For the first time in her short life, Doric looked at someone who wasn't afraid of her, and she hardly knew what to do with it.

"Well, if you decide you don't like it, we'll pick something else," Liavaris said. "But in the meantime, Doric, welcome to the Neverwinter Wood."

CHAPTER 15

Every member of the Emerald Enclave was assembled in the clearing, from the youngest druids to the oldest rangers, and all of those in between. The bells had stopped ringing now that everyone was assembled, but tension was running high, and the murmur of conversation swelled to a dull roar as they waited to find out what was happening. At last Kaliope walked to the front of the crowd, and Open lifted her up on top of a barrel.

"We have reports of a wildfire," Kaliope began, getting straight to the point. All other noise instantly stopped. "Word has been brought to us from a villager who lives on the edge of our pine forest. Their houses are threatened, and several other villages have already been consumed. The wind is blowing the fire towards us, and if we don't help put it out, this encampment will also burn."

Her declaration left no room for doubt in anyone's mind. The Enclave would have helped anyway, but with their own settlement under threat, they would waste no time.

"All of you know who you can follow," Kaliope said. "We don't have time to sort everyone into teams, so you're just going to have to do it yourselves. Gather whatever gear you need and prepare to leave immediately."

Doric looked towards Palanus and Open and realized with some horror that the other young druids were looking at *her*. She wanted to protest, but as Kaliope had said, there was no time. If they were going to follow her, she was going to have to lead. Hopefully Palanus would take over once they were ready to leave.

"We'll need any fire-resistant clothing you have," Doric said. She could withstand actual flame, but she needed sturdy clothing for it. Everyone else would need all the help they could get. "I don't think we'll need weapons, so don't bring anything big. Knives, in case you need to cut something free, and scarves to wrap around your mouth when it gets smoky."

They had been moving the whole time she was talking and split off to go to their quarters to pick up what she suggested. It was a matter of minutes before they had reassembled, and by then, Doric had located Palanus in the crowd again. Their instructor was with a bunch of senior druids, shepherding them along as they prepared to leave. Open was helping Kaliope pack a basket with various ointments and burn remedies. Everyone had a part to play.

It had taken Doric about half a day to walk from the village to the Enclave encampment the first time. Now, at speed, they all covered the ground much more quickly. The pine needles on the ground were dry, and the understory was primed for a fire. They would be in real trouble if the wind blew the flames in here. Forests needed fires, the same way people did, but a raging inferno would do no one any good.

After a couple hours of traveling quickly, they reached the edge of the forest. Some of the rangers had gone ahead to scout and were waiting for them with grim expressions on their faces.

"It's bad," Bramdain said. "This village is right in the fire's path, but there's another one to the north that's already in flames."

Doric watched as the villagers drove their sheep and cattle towards the river, hoping to escape with at least some of their livestock even if their fields and houses burned.

"Half of us will stay here," Kaliope said. "Send us what wounded you can, and we will start work on a firebreak. Arrhur will take anyone with fire resistance to the other village."

Doric started to move towards the dragonborn druid, but Gragwen grabbed her sleeve.

"We're coming with you," she said. She was still puffing for breath, having run to keep up.

"Gragwen," Doric began, but she could see by their faces that they would not be swayed. Even Leander was determined to go with her. "Fine, but someone will have to carry Jowenys's pack so that Gragwen can keep up."

Mistral took Jowenys's pack, Cassa took Gragwen's, and Jowenys hoisted Gragwen onto her shoulders. Arrhur was gathering everyone to him, and they scrambled to follow. Doric and Leander led the way, the only ones who weren't carrying extra gear until Doric made them stop and each take a package from Kaliope's collection of healing materials. They hurried after Arrhur as he led the mostly fire-resistant group onward.

It was a short walk over relatively even ground, but the smoke soon became almost intolerable. Doric wrapped her scarf around her face, which helped a little bit. Mistral would have created a small breeze to clear the air around them, but he was sure that would also fan the flames, so they just kept going. From Jowenys's shoulders, Gragwen had the best view, and it was she who spotted the burning houses first.

Arrhur didn't bother to issue orders, he simply waved the fire-resistant druids forward and plunged into a burning building himself. There were only about six of them, and as Doric pushed her way to the front of the group, she saw the few villagers who had managed to escape desperately looking back at their homes.

"We'll do what we can," she shouted over the noise of the burning and cracking wood. A villager looked at her and his eyes widened as she started moving through the fire. It was probably alarming to watch, especially since he had just escaped the inferno, but Doric couldn't waste time explaining to everyone that she could handle the flames.

"Be ready for wounded!" she called out. "And start getting water on the base of the flames."

She didn't look behind her, but she knew that they would start immediately. They had all improved since that day at the waterfall with Palanus, and not only could they send water anywhere they wanted, but they could also make it. The air was dry here, but the druids would wring whatever moisture they could from it.

Doric pushed her way into a burning house. The furniture was strewn all over the floor, as though someone had tripped over it while trying to get out. A man was lying on the floor, unconscious, and she knew that he had come back inside to save whoever was here. She could carry him, but she had to find the others first. She heard someone crying in one of the bedrooms and crossed the floor quickly. She kicked the door open and saw two little girls under the window, frantically trying to reach the latch to get it open.

"Come with me," Doric said. "Stay as low as you can, out of the smoke. Come, I will take you to your papa."

The girls were terrified, but they did what they were told. When they saw their father, they screamed, but Doric heaved him up onto her shoulders with considerable effort. She stumbled towards the door, hoping the girls were following her. They were over the threshold and back under the sky in a few moments, Doric's back straining under the weight. She took a few more steps, and then Jowenys was there, lifting the man away from her, while Gragwen took care of the children.

"Where—" Doric gasped for breath. "Where next?"

"The barn!" Jowenys yelled in her ear. "If you can let the animals out, they'll run away on their own."

Doric nodded and then turned back into the flames. The barn door was harder to open. The smell of straw overwhelmed her, and all she could think about was being trapped in an attic. There was no way her parents would have come back for her if the house had been on fire. It was irrational to be afraid: she wasn't a child anymore, and she was capable of withstanding fire, but she felt fear all the same.

A frantic lowing snapped her out of the memory, and Doric remembered what she had come here to do. She leapt into the barn and opened the door of every stall she passed. Some of the animals came out and made a break for it, but there were several she had to go back for and push out one at a time. The smoke clogged her lungs, but it was easier if she took her scarf off and wrapped it around their eyes. Then they had to trust that she was leading them to safety, and not farther into the flames. Finally, the barn was empty. A great cracking noise sounded, and Doric realized the roof was coming down. She threw herself clear of the building, and it crashed down, sending up more sparks and flaming embers into the air.

"Here," said Cassa, pushing a waterskin into her face. "It'll clear your throat."

Doric was expecting water, but instead it was some

sort of alchemical tincture. She drank as much as she could, feeling it soothe her throat. As a tiefling, she didn't burn, but the smoke was still irritating.

"What's next?" she asked when her voice returned. It was hoarse, but Cassa could hear her well enough.

"The fire has spread out into the woods," Cassa said. "The villagers are terrified that it'll wake up some monster there and that it will attack. I can't think of anything that lives in a forest and attacks burning towns, but they're frantic. There's no time to find Arrhur, and Leander has already gone to look. I think you should follow him. They've cleared almost all the buildings here."

Doric looked around and saw that it was true. There were many more villagers standing outside the circle of flames than there had been before, and the druids were mostly focused on putting water on the fire, not running into burning buildings.

"Tell Arrhur where we've gone," Doric said. Cassa nodded, and Doric took off into the woods.

The fire spread differently in the forest than it had in the town. Here, the mast burned greedily, knowing that it would seed when the flames went out. That didn't make life easier for Doric, though. She had Leander to worry about, and if the fire really did enrage some large animal, that wouldn't end well for anyone. She kicked herself for not asking Cassa more about where the monster lived. It was probably a cave. Doric saw a rocky outcrop in the distance and made for it. If it wasn't the cave she sought, she could climb it and try to get a better look.

In the distance, she thought she heard Leander yelling, but the flames were close behind her, and their roar was deafening. She hoped Leander was able to walk when she found him, because they were going to have a hard enough time getting out of here as it was. If she had to carry him through the growing flames, she would never let him forget it. She reached the outcrop and saw Leander was already there, but any relief she felt at seeing him on his feet was short-lived.

Just before she saw the cave, a loud screech rang out across the rocky ground. Doric looked around for the source of the noise. It wasn't any animal she was familiar with, though there was something that nagged at her about it, pieces she thought she should recognize. The screech sounded again, louder. There were deep reverberations under the sound, like there was a roar built into it. She could hear the scrape of claws on stone. Then the monster emerged from the cave. Doric wished she had brought more stones for her sling.

Owlbear.

CHAPTER 16

The most important thing to do in a fight was to not get distracted by thinking about things that were impossible. Owlbears were, obviously, possible, but a white owlbear was unlikely, and a white owlbear this far south was, well . . . Doric pushed past the denial, because the beast was clearly right in front of her, and therefore definitely not impossible. She looked at Leander, who seemed to be frozen on the spot. She had to get his attention somehow, let him know that she was here to help.

The owlbear stood at least ten feet high when it reared up on its hind legs, which it did as soon as it was free of the cave. Its face was more pointed than that of a regular bear. It didn't have teeth, but its hooked beak was probably the size of her head. Its talons were at least five inches long, curling towards razor-sharp points that scraped against the ground. The owlbear dropped to all four legs and charged straight towards Leander.

Doric saw his form ripple and knew what he was trying to do. It was probably better to run as an animal, so she didn't try to stop him. At the very last minute, she realized he was not trying to Wild Shape into one of the small, quick animals they had been practicing with. He was trying to become a bear, just like Doric's.

"No!" Doric shouted, but it was too late.

The owlbear didn't even check its speed as a giant bear appeared in front of it. Instead, it screeched again, defiant and furious, and slammed right into him.

Doric watched, frozen, as they grappled. For a moment, she thought that Leander would be all right. But inevitably the strain of fighting the owlbear and holding his Wild Shape was too much for him, and the bear disappeared. The owlbear didn't seem to notice and crushed him to the forest floor.

Doric whipped at the owlbear with thorns and called on the fire to aid her, but nothing she did could distract it from its prey. At least it was quick. Leander didn't even have time to scream. The owlbear turned its face to the sky and screeched in triumph. Then it seemed to remember that something else had been attacking it and turned to the spot where Doric stood.

Doric's first instinct was to run, but she knew that turning her back would be a mistake, just as much as turning into something big would be. Facing forward was only slightly better, but at least this way she could take in her surroundings and pick a spell before the owlbear sank its talons into her. What she needed most was time. She held up her hands, and a wall of stone rose up from the ground. The owlbear crashed into it at full speed and made another loud noise that walked the line between screech and roar. This close, Doric felt it in her bones.

The owlbear charged the wall again, but Doric held it. Her mind raced, looking for her next opening. The wall cracked the next time the owlbear hit it, but it was a sacrifice she had to make. She couldn't afford to waste precious minutes just standing there with the wall about to come down.

Doric waited until the wall was crumbling before she cast her next spell. This time, she Wild Shaped into the first bird she thought of and flew up to the branches of the closest tree. She was an owl with snowy white feathers that matched both the spirit who had protected her all those years ago and the beast that was currently trying to end her. The owlbear seemed a little bit stunned after bringing the wall down, but it still tracked her as she flew. This was all just buying time. She had to stop the creature from going to the village. She couldn't let what happened to Leander happen to anyone else.

The owlbear screeched again, which hurt the owl's ears even more than it had hurt Doric's regular ones. It shambled over to the tree, sank its talons into the bark, and shook the trunk. Doric held her wings out for balance, but it was only a matter of time. The flames were getting too close, and she was running out of options. She was going to have to fight the monster.

She threw herself off the branch, spreading soft wings as wide as she could before shifting again and plummeting towards the ground, directly above the owlbear. She landed right on top of it as a grizzly bear, still a bit smaller than the beast she was about to fight, but it was the biggest thing she could manage. She hoped she would be able to hold it longer than Leander had, or she would unquestionably meet his fate.

Now the owlbear was just angry. Taking the full weight of a falling grizzly was no joke, and even though Doric hadn't permanently disabled it, it still took a moment for it to shake her off. Doric rolled in the brush, coming up on all fours as the owlbear dropped down from its hind legs to charge her. She needed some sort of advantage to follow up with, so she turned into a lynx and ran towards the cave as fast as she could. Being inside the rock cavern would limit her range of motion, but it would limit the owlbear's even more. When the creature realized her destination, it picked up speed. Doric made it to the cave just ahead of it and had only seconds to assess everything before she plunged inside.

The cave was larger than she was expecting, with a rivulet of water streaming out of it from a burbling natural fountain towards the back. The owlbear had been nesting, bringing in all sorts of forest detritus to build, and digging into the guano to make a den. That was definitely something a monster would fight to protect.

She cursed—a feline growl that was rather satisfying in her mouth—and turned to face her opponent once again.

The owlbear had stopped outside the cave. It was panting for breath, and it seemed reluctant to follow her in, even to protect its nest. Now that she was no longer being attacked, Doric had time to look at the owlbear in more detail. It was young, she realized. It had gashes on its side that could have been made only by another owlbear's talons. One of its back claws was completely torn off. Doric and Leander were not the first big fight this creature had had, and it had not been victorious in the last one.

At the back of the cave was a ledge, too high for even the owlbear to reach. Doric shifted back to her tiefling shape and climbed up quickly. The owlbear shuffled into the cave. She tried to control her fear, but she couldn't forget the crunch of Leander's broken body against the earth. She forced herself to stop thinking about her friends and the fire and focus on the problem at hand.

"How did you get so wounded? Why are you here, so far away from home?" Doric asked, her voice low and calm. "Someone bigger than you drove you out, didn't they? You had nowhere to go, so you came south?"

She wasn't expecting an answer. She was mostly just reasoning through it out loud.

"Poor thing," she said, and pity swelled in her as she remembered Leander's last moments. Even if he had been a selfish bully, he didn't deserve to have his life cut short. "All you wanted was a nest, and you found the perfect cave, but there was a village too close by."

The owlbear came to the cave floor below the ledge and rose up on its hind feet again. Doric peered over the edge, a careful eye out for any swiping talons.

"You're not a monster at all," Doric said. "You're just scared and alone."

She felt something shift inside her as she said the words out loud, a realization so concrete that it changed something fundamental in her mind. *The owlbear wasn't a monster. It was just scared and alone.* Doric slid to the edge of her perch, making sure the owlbear could see her. Then she Wild Shaped.

Her owlbear was small, deliberately. She willed the white fur and feathers to match the wounded creature's and kept her beak and talons in proportion with her smaller form. When the other owlbear saw her, it reared back. When she slid down and let it get close, it calmed down. It sniffed her and preened some of the feathers on the back of her neck with its beak. Doric focused very hard on not screaming and running out of the cave. At last, the owlbear huffed, satisfied that she was not a threat.

The first problem was solved. Doric had calmed the beast. Now she just had to get it to go somewhere else, away from the fire and the villagers, who would un- doubtedly continue to harry it until it killed more of them. Doric rubbed her shoulder against the owlbear's side in what she hoped was an encouraging manner and started to walk out of the cave. For whatever reason, hopefully curiosity, the owlbear followed her.

Doric paused for a moment, looking around. They were very far from the owlbear's usual range, but if it had come all the way down here, it must not have been able to find anything closer to the ice. This couldn't be the only rocky outcrop in the area, surely. If Doric kept going, she could find another one that was properly isolated, and that could only work in the owlbear's favor. Doric knew she couldn't hold the shape forever, so she took up a quick pace, leading the way.

They made good time. The ground was rocky, which was a good sign, but there were hillocks of dirt with trees and shrubs on them. After that, the slopes increased, and the two of them had to go more slowly, but at least they were farther from the villages by then. The owlbear was ranging out on its own behind her, sniffing at trees and exploring its surroundings. Without the fire, it was even less of a danger, though she still needed to get it somewhere for everyone's safety. She hoped that she'd be able to leave it soon. She was exhausted, and she wanted to put some distance between them before she took her own shape again.

At last, the owlbear found a mossy hollow that suited it and began dragging pointy branches and sharp sticks out of its new nest. Doric watched until she was sure it was occupied and then, with the last bit of her strength, turned back into an owl and launched herself into a nearby tree. The owlbear missed her immediately, screeching mournfully, but it seemed to accept its isolation quickly and went back to work with a little less energy.

"Good luck," Doric said to herself.

Then she flew off on her soft wings, back the way she had come, until her strength failed her completely and she turned back into her usual form. She managed to land before she did, though only just, and her feet stumbled on the ground. Her pack was back where she'd first encountered the owlbear. So was Leander. She would have to get them both before she went back to the village.

DORIC STUMBLED BACK into the remnants of the village just before dawn, with Leander across her shoulders. The fire was out, but people were still busy tending to the wounded and making sure there weren't any flare-ups. It was a moment before someone looked up and saw them.

"Doric!" Open was running towards her, but not fast enough to catch her before she collapsed. He pulled Leander's body off her gently and helped her sit up. "Kaliope, I need you!"

Kaliope appeared with more of the tincture and something else for Doric's various scrapes and burns, which she hadn't even noticed picking up. Palanus gathered Leander's body in their arms and carried it over to where Arrhur was arranging the other dead.

"I changed," Doric gasped when her mouth was empty. "I know I promised I wouldn't, but I had to."

"It's okay," Open said. "When Palanus and I asked you to promise, we didn't imagine throwing you into a wildfire right away. I'm glad you could fight."

"I couldn't stop it." Doric's voice broke. "I couldn't stop it from killing Leander."

"Couldn't stop what?" Kaliope said.

"The monster!" one of the surviving villagers said. A murmur of agreement followed the statement. "She fought the monster! Did you kill it?"

Doric considered telling them she had, but if she did and one of them wandered into the owlbear's new nest, the whole cycle would start all over again.

"No." Doric gathered herself. "I drove it off. It's gone up into the hills. Just don't go up there and it won't bother you."

The villagers muttered angrily, but Palanus came back, and they quickly quieted down.

"You must focus on rebuilding," Palanus told them. "Not on some monster in the forest. You will need new houses by the time winter comes."

The villagers had to be satisfied with that.

"No more questions," Kaliope said as the young druids drew close. "She needs to sleep and rehydrate. You all do. We need to make our way home."

They moved slowly, Open helping Doric walk until she got her feet back under her. As Kaliope directed, the others left her alone. Doric was glad. She had a lot to think about. She hadn't told anyone what she had Wild Shaped into or what monster she had fought. She would have to figure out what to tell them. If turning into a bear was powerful and scary, then turning into an owlbear must be even worse.

The shift hadn't been entirely intentional, more instinctive. Palanus had said that instinct was fine but intention was something to replicate. She would have to practice. Alone. Even though she had done it in desperation and grief, it had been a wonderful feeling of power and strength. The rage and the precision. She would tell the others. Someday. She wanted to think her way through it before she did, though.

Doric did not remember the trip back to the Enclave encampment, but she did remember falling straight into her bed without taking off her grimy, smoky clothing. She'd have to wash the sheets to get the smell out, but for now it was worth it. All she wanted in the whole wide world was to sleep, and she hoped that by the time she woke up, everything would have sorted itself out.

In her dreams, she raced across a frozen landscape without feeling any cold, the ice crunching under her talons and the arctic wind blowing against her fur.

THE FIRST THING DORIC LEARNED ABOUT WOOD elves was that they were, as a general rule, nosy as hell.

The small wooden structure that Liavaris lived in had only one other bed. The old elf must have lived alone before Doric arrived, but ever since she woke up, there had been a steady stream of wood elves through the door. Some of them at least pretended to have other business with the elder, but most were there to look at Doric.

Doric looked right back.

Her hair was long and tangled, but her horns were clearly visible. Liavaris modified some trousers for her tail, so it was always on display as well. There was no hiding what she was, and Doric spent the first few days convinced they would throw her out, but they never did.

The little girl came in on the fourth day. She was small and slight, like all elf children, and she had dark-brown hair that was braided down her back. She was also sneaking, like a rabbit through the brush, no doubt about it. Liavaris had stepped out for some reason, and the girl tiptoed in the moment her back was turned, having clearly waited for the opportunity. She stopped in the center of the hut, staring at Doric like she hadn't thought her plan all the way through, and the truth was, she probably hadn't.

"Hello?" Doric said, like it was a question.

"Hello," the girl replied. She blinked a few times and didn't say anything else.

At least she wasn't screaming, like Doric's sister had. The wood elves had kept her so far, but if this girl was afraid, they'd probably get rid of her just like her father had.

"Did you need Liavaris for something?" Doric asked, even though the girl had clearly waited until the grown-up was gone.

"No," the girl said. "I was—I was wondering, you know, I just . . ."

Doric let her stumble through it.

"I wanted to see what the fuss was about," the girl said finally.

So there was a fuss. Doric hadn't heard raised voices, so Liavaris must have it under control, but they *were* arguing about her.

"What fuss?" Doric asked, because maybe this girl would tell her enough that she'd have a warning if she had to leave.

"Well." The girl paused. "Liavaris wants to keep you. And a couple of the elders are not sure she should."

She knew it would happen, but it still hurt.

She wouldn't return to the river. She'd find a more secure place to set up her next camp.

"Liavaris's going to win," the girl said. "My mother says so, and she's not wrong very often."

Doric wondered what it was like to have that much faith in the people around you. She barely trusted Liavaris, and she had no reason to trust anyone else.

"Anyway, I'm Torrieth," the girl said. "I'm eight, so I think I'm only a little bit older than you. I can teach you whatever you need to know about the forest, and when you're all caught up, we can be hunting partners."

Now it was Doric's turn to blink. She knew how to hunt, and she had already survived in the forest. After a moment, she realized that what Torrieth really meant was that she wanted to spend time with her.

"Not that we'd be hunters yet," the older girl continued as though nothing were strange. "We'd have to be apprentices first, but my point is, if you're my partner, I won't have to spend so much time with my cousins, because they are *the worst*."

"All right," Doric agreed. She didn't really feel like she had a choice in the matter, as Torrieth had clearly decided. Plus, this would give her a purpose. And, just maybe, another companion.

"Excellent," Torrieth said. "Have you ever fired a bow?"

She reached out and grabbed Doric's hand before Doric had time to respond. She was so surprised she didn't even flinch, and Torrieth drew the hand up close to inspect it.

"No calluses, so you haven't, I guess," Torrieth said. She let go, and Doric put her hand in her lap, still kind of stunned. "But if you managed to live all this time by yourself in the woods, you must be a quick learner. This will be perfect."

There was a noise at the front of the hut, and then Liavaris walked back in. Doric looked back and forth between the old elf and the young one, but Torrieth didn't look at all worried about being caught in the act.

"So I see you two have met," Liavaris said, amusement in her eyes.

"Doric is going to be my hunting partner," Torrieth told her. "I know she's a bit younger, but with my help, she'll catch up in no time. We are going to be the best."

"I don't doubt it," Liavaris said. "Do you intend to start tomorrow, or were you going to let Doric finish healing first?"

Torrieth giggled. It was a nice sound, like river water over rocks. Doric liked it, though she wasn't sure she would ever be able to make such a sound herself.

"We'll wait," Torrieth said. "Can I help?"

Liavaris looked between them again, measuring and liking what she saw.

"I don't imagine it's very exciting for Doric in

here by herself," Liavaris said. "If it's all right with her, you can stay and tell her about our camp. There's a lot to learn, and you're as good as anyone else to tell her about it."

Torrieth looked at Doric, clearly hoping that Doric would say yes. Doric was perplexed but not about to refuse. Torrieth must *really* want a hunting partner who wasn't one of her as-yet-unseen cousins.

"I don't mind," Doric said.

"We're going to have so much fun," Torrieth promised.

Beyond all reason, Doric believed her.

CHAPTER 17

It was well after sunrise by the time Doric hauled herself into the kitchen the day after the wildfire. Or maybe two days after the wildfire. She had slept almost a whole day and night, and she still wasn't awake enough to properly count the passing of time. Even now, she didn't really want to get out of bed, but the smell of food was too enticing. She was alone in the room. Jowenys had left her a basin full of water, so Doric was able to wash and put on clean clothes before she faced the world.

"I made pancakes," Open said when he saw her.

This turned out to be an understatement. If someone had asked her, she might have said that Open had made every single pancake in the entire world. The table was covered with stacks of them, along with fruit and cream and more of the pinecone syrup Doric was coming to like. Her stomach almost rebelled on the spot.

"I also made toast," Open said after a look at her face.

She sat down, and he set a plate of toast in front of her along with butter and salt. She ate the first two pieces mechanically, but by the time she started on the third, she was beginning to feel better.

"Where are the others?" she asked. It was much too quiet.

"They're outside," Open said. "Palanus is holding a vigil for anyone who wishes to attend."

Doric immediately tried to get up from the table, and Open pushed her back down.

"You are supposed to eat at least one thing from every food group before you go outside," Open said. "And Kaliope left some kind of tonic for you in the kitchen. Will you be all right if I go get it?"

Doric nodded and dutifully added several slices of apple, a hunk of cheese, and two sausages to her plate. It didn't look like anyone had actually eaten the pancakes. She felt a little bad.

"Cooking makes me feel better, and pancakes can take a long time if you make enough of them," Open said, sitting back down and passing her a small bottle. "Making them was all I really needed. If no one eats them, then the pigs will be very happy."

Doric poured the contents of the bottle down her

throat without tasting them, then went to work on the sausage and cheese.

"Did you see it?" Open asked gently. "The creature the villagers were afraid of?"

"Yes," she said. "But then I couldn't save him when he tried to fight it."

Open blew out a gust of air like a sigh wasn't big enough.

"I could tell you that it happens," he said. "That it happens to all of us, because it does in this type of life. But there's nothing I can say that will make you feel better."

"When I got the creature to leave, I felt proud of myself," Doric confessed. "I felt like I had done a good job. I remembered Leander, but there was a moment where I was actually happy about helping it get to a better home."

Open looked at her shrewdly, like he knew that she was leaving significant details out of her story, but he didn't push her.

"The only thing that will help is moving on to the next task, and doing a better job of it," he said. He stood up. "When you're done with your breakfast, come outside."

Doric ate as quickly as she could, but every swallow was a fight. Here she was at a fully laden breakfast table, and Leander was dead. He'd gone to fight a fire and ended up fighting an owlbear. Even though neither of those things was directly her fault, she had a sneaking suspicion he'd jumped at the chance to face "the monster" on his own. If she hadn't Wild Shaped into a bear in the first place, they might all be sitting here, and the pancakes would actually get eaten.

She tucked an apple into her pocket in case she got hungry later and headed outside. A few of the druids and other Enclave members were going about their morning tasks, but most of them were over on the far side of the clearing. Doric made her way over. It was easy to spot Jowenys in the crowd, so Doric sat beside her. The others were there, too. Cassa's eyes were red and puffy.

"He was a jerk," she said. "But he was still, you know."

Doric did know.

Palanus rose gracefully to their feet and bent to pick something up off the ground. When they stood up, Doric could see that it was actually two somethings: one of Kaliope's garden spades and a small oak sapling. Without a word, Palanus went to the edge of the clearing and dug a small hole into the loamy soil there. They planted the sapling, patting the dirt firmly around the nascent roots.

"When we live, we grow, and when we die, we grow," Palanus said. "Your body may lie far away, Leander, buried with the others who shared your fate in the wildfire, but we will remember you here as this tree grows ever taller."

When they were done, those assembled began to drift away from the gathering. Some went back to their tasks, while a few others went to the sapling and poured a little bit of water on it. Open arrived beside Doric just as the group was standing up and handed her a waterskin. She nodded and led the way over to the sapling. One by one, each of them poured a bit of water—not so much that the roots would flood, but enough that they would dig deep and grow.

"I think I'd like to go for a walk," Doric said as they moved away. "By myself."

Jowenys chewed on her lip, clearly ready to talk about what had happened, but Mistral and Gragwen nodded. Remigold was patting Cassa on the shoulder.

"All right," he said. "Don't be gone too long. We need to see each other today, even if we're not talking."

Doric turned away from them and headed into the forest. She felt better the instant she stepped into the shade of the trees. The scent of pine filled her nostrils, but it didn't evoke the memory of fire. She walked faster, pushing herself to keep the quick pace as she put distance between herself and the encampment.

She would tell Open about the owlbear. He would understand. She hoped. Jowenys or any of the rest of them would think it was strange at the very best, and she didn't trust any of the senior druids. Even Palanus already thought her Wild Shape was too much, and that was without knowing that she could change into a monster.

The owlbear wasn't a monster. She knew it like she knew her name and the path of the sun, but she didn't think anyone else would feel the same way. They would just see Doric: the tiefling druid who couldn't control her temper and now could also turn into a creature that any normal person would avoid. Open might understand that. He had fought for acceptance, too. And he might forgive her for not killing it, even though it had killed Leander.

She was so focused on putting space between herself and the encampment that she didn't notice that someone was shadowing her until he got very close.

"You know," he said conversationally, "I really thought a large camp of druids would be easier to find."

Doric had a stone in her sling before she knew she was moving. A boy was next to her in the middle of the woods, his hands up to show he carried nothing dangerous, and a confused expression on his face.

"Doric, it's me," he said. "Simon? The sorcerer? I was at that village? With the well? It was a whole bonding thing, I thought, but, uh, maybe not."

"I have no idea who you are," Doric said. She racked her brain trying to remember. He'd been standing in a pond, probably.

"That's fine, I guess. Obviously, I have been through a lot since the last time we spoke." The boy—Simon—sighed. Doric didn't have the faintest idea what he was talking about. Some of his clothing was singed.

"Were you in the fire?" she asked.

"Sort of," he said. "I mean, I was in the village, and it was definitely on fire. I tried to help, but the cat I rescued was really clingy. She would not let me out of her—You know, I really just wanted to tell you that I thought you did a good job talking to those villagers after the fire was out. I get all wobbly when someone yells at me."

"I didn't enjoy it," Doric told him. "I just did what I had to."

"And you took care of the monster?" Simon asked.

"It wasn't a monster," Doric said. The response came automatically, an answer to the feeling inside her that she knew down to her marrow was the truth. "It was an owlbear."

Simon stared at her. She met his gaze, and he dropped his eyes almost immediately. She hadn't meant to tell anyone, and here she was telling someone she barely knew.

"Owlbears are pretty big," he said. "Did you fight it with that?"

He gestured to the sling, which Doric realized she still had loaded. She tucked the stone away in her belt pouch and relaxed.

"No," she said. "I used magic."

She didn't feel like telling him all the details. Kaliope said that sorcerers could sometimes be very annoying about spells—though not as bad as wizards—and Doric had no desire to get involved in an academic discussion about how her magic worked.

"I can't really use magic for very much," Simon admitted. "Not reliably, anyway."

"You said you were a sorcerer," Doric countered. She would have guessed he was older than she was. Surely, he must have been practicing longer.

"Well, yes," Simon said. "I'm a sorcerer in that I can theoretically do some spells. Just not a lot of them. And not very often."

"That's a little sad," Doric said. She instantly wondered if that was too insulting.

"I know," Simon replied. He seemed to be a realist.

"I'll keep practicing. Just maybe not in the middle of wildfires. I'll get better eventually."

Doric wondered why she had run into him again, even though she barely remembered running into him the first time. Liavaris didn't believe in accidents, but for the life of her, Doric could not think of a single reason she needed to know this boy.

"I should get back to camp," Doric said.

"Oh, don't let me keep you," Simon said. "I'm not staying here, which is too bad because I would love to talk some more with you. I have some important errands to run. Somewhere else. But we've already met twice! Maybe we shall meet again."

Doric mumbled something she hoped was polite and set off through the forest by herself. When she looked back, Simon was watching her. It wasn't creepy or anything, it was just weird. He was just weird. They would probably never see each other again. Maybe she should have invited him back for lunch. But that would have involved too much explaining. He didn't seem offended, and this way, she could put him out of her mind immediately. When she looked back again, he was gone.

CHAPTER 18

None of them slept well the night after the vigil. They had spent the afternoon sitting listlessly around the encampment, and not even Kaliope's enforced threats of carrying water to the garden were enough to tire them out. Doric knew that Jowenys was awake above her, but she couldn't bring herself to talk. She just lay on her bunk, absently tracing the lines of wax that Jowenys had used to plug up the wall.

In the morning, they arrived at breakfast to find steaming bowls of porridge laced with dark brown sugar and a powdery spice that Palanus traded for whenever they had the opportunity. The half-orc ate it in its normal form, which was much like tree bark, but the rest of them ate the ground-up version. Doric had eaten one piece of the bark and sneezed for an hour, so she switched to smaller portions after that. Just a little on her porridge or sprinkled into a hot drink was enough for her.

If the meal was meant to comfort them, it did. Unlike the mountain of pancakes the day before, this was a normal, everyday kind of meal. It made things seem easier, even though nothing had really improved.

Breakfast passed quickly, and then, instead of going outside, they gathered around the hearth in the common area. Several older druids had come into the cabin for some of Open's cooking that morning, and now they were sitting around telling stories. Some of them were simply too outrageous to be true, but some of them were surprisingly useful.

"And the thieves were caught," wound up one of the stories, "but mark my words, we haven't heard the last of them. A barbarian and a bard? Who knows what kind of mischief they can stir up, even from prison."

Doric disregarded the story, but as the days went on, the old druid told it again and again. The tale involved a pair of unreasonably prolific thieves who seemed to be completely unstoppable, except for the part where they'd been caught and thrown in prison. No one knew all the details, and no one seemed to care, except that there was a magical item that none of them would talk about that no one seemed to know the location of.

The seasons marched on. The neighboring villages brought the harvest in, and the druid initiates studied the changes to a forest in the fall. They foraged for pine nuts, which was new to Doric since the predominant seed in the Neverwinter Wood was acorns. Each initiate grew stronger and more capable, though they still had to work hard to succeed as much as Palanus pushed them to.

One morning, soon after the forest had been locked in snow, Open came into the great room after disappearing to the kitchen to tidy up after lunch. He took a seat by the fire and cleared his throat so that they all looked in his direction.

"Doric, there's a message for you," he said.

"From the human village?" Doric asked, her heart sinking. Whether it was the owlbear returning unexpectedly or something less directly her fault, she didn't want more bad things to happen to that town.

"No," Open said. "It's from the Neverwinter Wood."

Doric crossed the room in a flash, heedless of the watching druids. She took the bundle from Open. It hadn't been opened, which was nice. Her name and location were scratched on the outside, along with some wax, a set of claw marks, and the stamp from the post office down by the river.

Open stood and let her have his seat, even though he'd just arrived. He went off to collect teacups while she made herself comfortable in the large chair. Her feet swung off the floor, which always made her feel foolish.

"Dear Doric," she read. "We hope this letter finds you. We weren't sure exactly how to address it, but the druid I spoke to by the name of Ash said that this should be sufficient.

"I wish I had better news for you, but the truth is that the logging camps like the one you and Torrieth found in the spring have only grown in number. The humans have shown no signs of leaving. They have already redirected one river, and we see no reason why they won't make further mistakes.

"We were hoping we could request your aid. We need it. I have put off writing this letter long enough, despite Torrieth's encouragement. Hopefully you will make good time traveling and we will see you soon. Please send word if there is not to be a druid response so that we can come up with another solution.

"Yours affectionately, Liavaris."

Doric read the letter twice, a hard feeling in her chest. She had hoped Marlion was right about the humans, even though she had believed the opposite. Moreover, she had hoped to make a triumphant return to the forest as a druid in her own right, not to be summoned home on the off chance that she could help or bring someone who could. It was undeniably nice to be wanted. Being useful to the wood elves was a large part of the reason she had come here to train. But she had let her guard down and become accustomed to people liking her just because they finally did. Liavaris's request hurt, even though it shouldn't have, and then Doric felt guilty for feeling hurt, when it was clearly an emergency. She had so many feelings she thought her chest might cave in.

"Doric?" Jowenys said. "Is everything okay?"

"No," Doric said. Her voice was hoarse, like her throat was full of rocks. "I need to go home."

She passed the letter to Kaliope, who read it quickly and passed it on to Palanus. Both of her teachers had grave expressions on their faces when they finished reading.

"You have our permission," Kaliope said. "But it's not a short trip, Doric. You could be gone for months. We can teleport you some of the way, but you'll still have to stay in the Neverwinter area for a while to deal with the issue."

"I'll go with her," Jowenys said.

Palanus looked at her, a measuring expression on their face. Jowenys didn't so much as flinch.

"If you leave, it might be half a year, Jowenys," Kaliope said. "And the portal only goes in one direction. You'd have to make the return journey the long way."

Jowenys looked back and forth between Doric and the others. She blinked several times, but then she raised her chin.

"I understand," Jowenys said.

Doric knew better than to fight with her about it in front of everyone else. There would be time for that later.

"Come on, Doric," Open said. "Even teleporting, you'll need to pack. Let's take a look at your gear and see what needs replenishing."

"Thank you," Doric said as Jowenys walked past her on her way to pack.

"You'd do it for me," Jowenys said. "Well, you might not think of it so quickly, but you'd get there eventually, and that's what matters."

Doric smiled, and if Jowenys's smile was a little watery, neither of them commented on it.

They spent the afternoon preparing. Doric had meant to tell Open the truth about the owlbear encounter, but it kept sticking in her throat. Now that she was about to leave, she thought it might be the perfect time, but still something held her back. The wood elves were hoping for a druid, powerful and controlled. The owlbear was powerful, but Doric didn't think it was controlled—and maybe it couldn't be.

"Open," she said when it was just the two of them in the kitchen packing rations. "I have to tell you something about the creature that killed Leander. It was an owlbear."

"We knew you were leaving something out," Open said. "I'm glad you decided to tell me. Did you kill it by accident?"

"No," Doric said. "I . . . I Wild Shaped into one. That's how I got it to follow me. It followed another owlbear."

"Doric," Open said. He leaned on his elbows, surprise written on his features and a bit of alarm in the back of his eyes. "That's imposs—"

"I can't explain it," Doric said quickly, before he could finish the word. "I just did it."

She could barely meet his gaze. She was afraid of what she'd see. She didn't want more power; she wanted the power she had to be tamed.

"We'll talk about it when you get back," Open said. His voice sounded strained. For the first time since she'd met him, his face looked closed.

Doric fled the kitchen without looking at him again, thinking she'd disappointed him by being so unpredictable. She avoided him for the rest of the afternoon.

Dinner was almost merry, though if she was being honest with herself, Doric felt like her emotional equilibrium had burned up in the fire. There were quiet moments when everyone remembered that Leander had died. Soon many of the senior druids joined them at the table, and they were a raucous bunch after a few cups of mead. They told stories and sang songs, and it was the closest thing they'd had to a party since Doric had arrived at the Enclave. Eventually, one of the visiting bards started playing, and then the room descended into mayhem as the dancing started.

Doric kept to the sidelines. The Emerald Enclave had people from all over the world as its members, and each of them seemed to have their own kind of dance. There was laughter and a great many collisions.

"This is how it is, too," Palanus said, appearing beside her. They didn't look like they wanted to dance either. "For every bad night, there are more nights like this."

Doric knew it was their way of comforting her, so she let herself feel a little better. She even laughed when Cassa tried to teach Gragwen a human reel, only for both of them to wind up nearly flattened by three dragonborn and a tabaxi doing the polka.

It was very late by the time she and Jowenys were getting ready for what would be their last night of sleep with the Enclave for a while.

"We can do this, Doric," she said. "They're getting two druids for the price of one."

Jowenys took her hand, and Doric forced a smile onto her face. It would get easier with time. Tonight was for celebrating. Tomorrow, she would face the world.

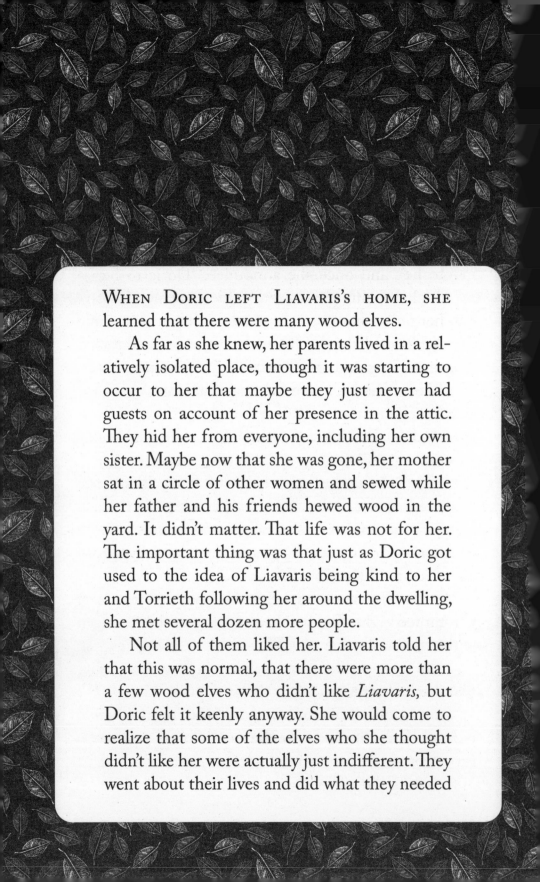

When Doric left Liavaris's home, she learned that there were many wood elves.

As far as she knew, her parents lived in a relatively isolated place, though it was starting to occur to her that maybe they just never had guests on account of her presence in the attic. They hid her from everyone, including her own sister. Maybe now that she was gone, her mother sat in a circle of other women and sewed while her father and his friends hewed wood in the yard. It didn't matter. That life was not for her. The important thing was that just as Doric got used to the idea of Liavaris being kind to her and Torrieth following her around the dwelling, she met several dozen more people.

Not all of them liked her. Liavaris told her that this was normal, that there were more than a few wood elves who didn't like *Liavaris*, but Doric felt it keenly anyway. She would come to realize that some of the elves who she thought didn't like her were actually just indifferent. They went about their lives and did what they needed to do but stuck to themselves without interacting with too many people at all. Those she could handle. The elves that hated her on sight were another matter. For now, Doric avoided them and hoped that they never decided to complain about her.

The younger wood elves were fascinated with her. Torrieth had a sort of bullheadedness to her, and once she announced Doric to her circle of elflings, no one said anything about her tail or her horns. In fact, no one ever really mentioned them. She was a wood elf as far as they were concerned. A weird one maybe, but Liavaris had adopted her, so Doric was a part of the clan.

For the first few years, Doric kept a bag packed and some supplies hidden in rotted-out trees surrounding the settlement. If Liavaris knew about it, she didn't say anything. Torrieth definitely didn't know. She would be offended. Doric was slowly feeling safer amongst the wood elves, but by no means was she comfortable.

It all came to a head the year that Doric turned eight. She had been sitting in the forest, watching for her owl. She hadn't seen the creature since the flood and was starting to wonder if she had imagined it in the first place. She was sitting on a stump, leaning forward so that her tail hung off the back. The two hunters passing through the brush on their way home for the evening did not see her.

"She hasn't caused any problems," one said.

Doric listened out of habit.

"Aye, so you've mentioned," said the other. "The children love her, and Liavaris won't hear a word against her. I just don't like it, that's all."

Doric froze, willing herself to become part of the dead tree.

"Look, I know that it's considered unnatural, what she is," the first elf said, "but she's a child."

"A child who managed to live in the forest by herself," the second pointed out. "How is that natural?"

"I'm not saying she isn't lucky," the first elf said. "I'm just saying that I'm not about to turn away a little girl, no matter what she looks like."

"And when she's grown?" the second elf demanded.

In the long silence that followed, Doric lived and died a thousand times. She saw her future spooling out in front of her, variations on a theme. The wood elves kept her. The wood elves drove her away. The wood elves let her remain but made her life hard. The wood elves forced her out of the forest entirely, banishing her from her home for the second time in her life.

"I suppose we'll see," said the first elf.

Doric stayed sitting on the stump as they walked by. She couldn't tell who was talking, and that was both better and worse. She didn't know who had it in for her, but at the same time, she would have to second-guess every word from every hunter going forward. She wished it had been raining today so that she could have stayed inside. She wished she had gone to play with Torrieth, who would have said something, even to a pair of grown-ups.

As if in answer to her thoughts, Torrieth stumbled out of the brush, talking a mile a minute about something one of the boys had found in the creek. Tadpoles were just as confused about the weather here as anything else, so these frogs had apparently grown to be enormous, and Doric must come and see them right away. Doric let Torrieth take her hand and lead her away from the camp, still talking about whether it was worth the risk to tuck one of the frogs into her sister's bed. Doric couldn't imagine doing something like that. She couldn't possibly risk it. Yet Torrieth talked as though it would be funny, and even if her sister screeched at her, they would all laugh about it later.

Doric did her best to play along. She caught a frog. She held it threateningly close to Deverel's head while everyone squealed, both fascinated and horrified.

The owl never came.

CHAPTER 19

Before they left, Doric gave Open the last of the horn paste that Liavaris had made for her. As far as Doric knew, he didn't have anything to stop his horns from itching, though he never complained.

"Thank you," he said after taking a delicate sniff.

"I don't know if it'll make a difference for you," Doric said. "But . . . well, it was good not being the only one, the only tiefling, while I was here. I know you didn't make everyone be nice to me, but you treated me like being a tiefling was normal, and I didn't know what that was like."

"I understand completely," Open said. "That's why I almost never venture far from here. This is my home.

Here, the druids are used to us. But even Palanus faces some difficulties when they venture out into the world. I admire you, Doric."

She didn't mean to, but she definitely turned a little pink under his praise. The subject of the owlbear hung heavily between them, even though he didn't bring it up again. They didn't have time. But it would hurt a lot if she lost his approval. Maybe this was a sign that she could earn it back.

"Make sure Jowenys doesn't push herself too hard," Open said. "You know she'll do anything for you."

"I'll keep an eye out," Doric said.

Open smiled.

"When you're done, if you want to come back, you're always welcome, you hear?" he offered.

"She hears you," Kaliope said. "Now let's get these girls on their way before we both start crying."

Doric pulled her cloak tightly around her body and followed Jowenys and Palanus into the brisk forest air. The plan was that Palanus would take them a ways up-river and then send them through a portal that they knew of near Waterdeep. They still needed a ship, though. Doric hoped that she'd see Captain Dartha's ship when they made it to the river, but she wasn't sure she was that lucky. When she actually saw the familiar mast in the middle of the river with all the others, she thought that something was finally going her way.

When they got closer, Doric started to have second thoughts.

"We'll have her patched up in a jiffy," said Dartha as he watched several crew members patch a rather large hole in the hull. "Hit a damn iceberg on the way in. Above the waterline, or we'd all be bobbing out there with them. Didn't even take on that much water."

He seemed confident, but Doric could tell that Jowenys had moved past second thoughts into thirds.

"The river is full of ice!" Jowenys protested. "What will the ocean be like?"

"It's an annual thing," Dartha said casually. "We'll be past it in no time. There's nothing to worry about."

"If he says it's fine, it's fine," Doric said. "When will you be ready to leave?"

"We've only just set the seam, so it'll be a while," Dartha said. "But you might as well come aboard. That way, we'll be ready to go as soon as it dries."

Doric pulled Jowenys up the gangway by the end of her cloak.

"I don't like sailing," Jowenys said.

"You might have said something before," Doric told her.

"I was busy being all noble and volunteering to go with you on your quest," Jowenys said. Despite what she claimed, she was steady enough on her feet as the water rolled beneath them. "I wasn't really thinking about the practicalities."

Doric shrugged. "It might be fun."

A giant piece of ice hit the other side of the ship, a solid-sounding thump reverberating through the air. Palanus breathed out a heavy sigh.

It wasn't very much fun.

JOWENYS FORGAVE HER for everything once her feet were back on solid ground. Dartha had taken them on the shortest crossing possible, and Jowenys had been sick with worry almost the entire time. The ice had been quite a bit more than Dartha had implied. Their sailors were skilled, but the sea was still the sea and couldn't be predicted. Even Doric was a little queasy sometimes. They were still with Palanus, but it was time for the real part of the adventure to begin.

Palanus took them to the portal location. There were sites like it across the realms. There was even one nearer to the Enclave encampment, but its use was highly regulated by one of the merchant guilds, and since time was of the essence, they were using this one. The portal would take them to a corresponding portal that was close to the Neverwinter Wood. They would land near the city of Neverwinter itself, but outside the walls. Then they would journey northeast to the forest.

Palanus activated the portal, channeling power through an oak tree that marked the spot. The air shimmered, and Doric thought she could see things on the other side.

"Does it hurt?" asked Jowenys.

"It tickles a bit," Palanus told her.

Doric wasn't sure if they were kidding. She made sure her pack was secure and nodded at their teacher. Then she stepped through the portal. It did tickle, but it was over so quickly that she barely noticed. She materialized near unfamiliar walls but could tell by the lack of bite in the air that they were in Neverwinter. A breath later, Jowenys appeared beside her, and the portal closed.

"I'm moving here," Jowenys announced, checking her arms and legs to make sure everything was where it was supposed to be, her face turned to the sun. "I am moving here, and I am never leaving, ever again."

Doric checked herself as well, even though she knew it was silly. She had to admit, it was nice not to see her breath before her face every time she exhaled.

"I can probably set you up somewhere," Doric said. "But I think you'd get bored after a while."

"I'll manage," Jowenys said.

She picked up her pack from where it lay beside Doric's feet and set off at a steady pace.

Even on foot, they made good time. The sun had been right overhead when they exited the portal, and before it set, Doric could see one of the familiar villages that huddled around the forest fringe.

"Is that them?" Jowenys asked, her voice low.

"No," Doric said. "Those woodcutters have always been here. They farm the trees, not quite like druids do, but they make sure to plant new ones as they cut. They aren't wasteful. They only take certain-sized logs. We can camp on the other side of the village if you like."

"There's a tavern," Jowenys said, a note of adventure in her voice. "I've always wanted to stay in a tavern."

Doric gave her a hard look.

"Come on, I know we're in a hurry, but we have to stay somewhere," Jowenys said. "This way we won't have to strike camp in the morning! We can just get up and leave."

Doric sighed.

THE VILLAGE WASN'T much. Fewer than a dozen houses clustered around a well. Some of the houses were clearly for people other than woodcutters since they didn't have axes and saws hanging from the porch rafters, which meant this village was doing pretty well. Doric and Jowenys walked towards the biggest house, getting close enough to read the sign that hung out in front of it. *The Gauntlet and Grinder.* Doric didn't imagine it was anything fancy, but Jowenys looked excited.

Inside the tavern it was dim. A wooden bar stretched along one side of the wall, with two humans and a dwarf bustling behind it, filling tankards. Several customers sat at the bar itself, and a few others lounged at tables around the room. The walls were made of dark wood, and the lanterns didn't do much to light the place. It was dark, but it was a friendly sort of darkness. Like the owlbear welcoming her into its new den.

"What'll you have?" said the dwarf. She had a tankard in one hand and a cloth in the other.

"Uh," Doric said. She hadn't exactly thought this through. Apparently Jowenys hadn't either, because she remained uncharacteristically quiet. Doric did have some money in her belt, though. "A pint?"

The dwarf laughed, not unkindly.

"Everyone had a first time in a tavern, loves," she said. "Let's start you with a half pint."

They didn't argue. The tankard that was placed in front of Doric was smaller than the one the dwarf had been carrying and looked much more manageable. It was made of wood, held together the same way a barrel was, and only a slow seepage of ale showed any flaws in its construction.

Doric slowly drank her ale while Jowenys coughed and carried bravely on. The tavern filled up as the night got darker. Most of the people were humans, but there were a few dwarves and orcs in the mix. All of them seemed to work together. There were so many conversations going on around them that Doric couldn't follow them all. The dwarf barkeep refilled her tankard—Jowenys wasn't done yet—but instead of the light-headedness that Cassa had warned her about with ale, all Doric felt was a bloated stomach.

Jowenys struck up a conversation with two dwarves sitting at the next table. From the expression on her face, Doric would have assumed that she was raptly listening to some grand and exciting adventure. Instead, the dwarves were talking about how to make sure trees grew straight trunks so that they could be cut into planks for building ships. Doric smiled in spite of herself and tapped Jowenys on the shoulder.

"I'm going to find the privy," she said.

"Okay," said Jowenys, and turned back to the dwarves.

She got up and went to look for the privy. It was attached to the tavern, but you still had to go outside to get there, which prevented the smell from getting through. Doric pushed the door open and entered a room with no light at all, save for what came in from the crack between the top of the wall and the overhanging roof. It took a moment of blinking for her eyes to adjust.

Someone was crying.

Doric made her way to the back wall, where there were two stalls and an extremely dingy piece of bronze that might have been meant to be a mirror. The crying girl was in one of the stalls. Doric wasn't entirely sure of the protocol here, but she didn't feel comfortable not offering to help. Before she could think of what to say, the door behind her burst open, and several more young women piled into the bathroom.

"Bethda, are you in here?" one of them demanded.

There was a sniffling noise, and then, "Yes," came the answer through the stall door.

"Oh, Bethda, I'm so sorry," the girl said, immediately walking over and leaning against the door. "I know you really liked him, but he's not worth this."

Doric really needed to use the toilet, but there seemed to be a moment developing, so she stayed where she was.

"You know what we should do," a second girl said, clearly not expecting an answer. "We should go to his house and cover it with egg yolk."

"Also a waste," said a third girl. "I'm not giving up my egg money for a whole week just to make a mess that he probably won't even clean up."

"Bastard," said the first girl. "Bethda, you have to come out of there. If nothing else, I think someone is waiting for the stall."

"I can use the other one," Doric whispered, but the

girl waved her to silence. "I mean, yes. I would like to, if you don't mind."

Bethda blew her nose, and then the stall door opened. Doric nodded cheerfully at her, even though neither of them felt it, and went in to do her business. She heard the pump handle squeak as someone got water for Bethda to clean up. The girls were still plotting revenge when Doric came out to wash up.

"Ugh," said the first girl. "I want to tear him to pieces with my bare hands."

Doric stilled at the word, even though she knew it wasn't exactly what the girl had meant. She leaned over the stream of water that came out of the pump. Wasn't this what the Enclave did? Help? These girls were strangers, strange humans at that. She could help them and then walk away. Jowenys was busy. It was only her.

"You know," she said as casually as possible. Outside the stall, there was enough light that they would see her druidic armor. "If you wanted, I could tear him to pieces with my bear hands."

Bethda looked at her. Doric's hood had fallen back, and she hadn't picked her tail up yet. She blinked a couple of times, and Doric realized that this was what Cassa was talking about with regard to ale.

"You're scary," Bethda said. She looked Doric up and down, not flinching when she saw the horns. "I like that."

The first girl linked elbows with Bethda and led everyone back outside. Doric followed, willing to see how far she could go with them before they turned on her. In the twilight, it was much easier to see what her new companions looked like. They were all human girls around her age. They were dressed in plain but sturdy-looking tunics over wide-legged trousers. Skirts weren't entirely practical here, Doric guessed, especially in the woods.

"I'm Sara," said the girl. "You've met Bethda. She has unfortunate taste, but in her defense, it is very boring here. Those two are Isla and Laress. What were you saying about a bear?"

Doric looked around. The girls seemed eager, but there were too many houses too close together. Through the tavern window, she spotted Jowenys, still deep in conversation with the dwarves. It felt reckless, but these girls weren't afraid of her. Jowenys wouldn't even miss her if they were quick.

"You'd better come with me," Doric said. "This is a little hard to explain."

She led the way past the last house. Sara had grabbed a torch on their way out of the village, and it didn't make a huge difference, but Doric wasn't about to protest. She had never thought to ask about druid rules on showing off. Surely, this was balance, too. Bethda was miserable, and someone should make that right.

"I promise you, I am not dangerous, so you don't need to scream," Doric said. "Don't drop that torch."

The girls murmured something about not being afraid, and Sara gripped the torch more tightly. Doric wasn't sure that was going to work, but she had done all she could to warn them. She hadn't tried to turn into the owlbear since the day of the wildfire. And now she was about to reveal herself to a bunch of drunk human girls. She could feel Palanus's sigh, but they weren't here, so she didn't have to listen to them.

Doric reached inside herself to the place that knew the owlbear was not a monster. It was still there, as firm in belief as ever. She wrapped herself around that feeling and allowed her form to change.

"Gods . . ." Sara said. She didn't drop the torch.

Bethda and Isla took a few steps back, and Laress did let out a tiny scream, but she clapped her hand over her mouth before it got too far.

"You do have bear hands," Bethda said. "Owly bear hands! Neat!"

Doric gestured that they should lead her to wherever they wanted her to go. Sara passed the torch over to Isla and drew a small shortsword out from under her coat.

"Just in case," she said, though that was alarmingly nonspecific.

Sara led the way around the village, to the house of the boy who had been mean to Bethda. It was on the far side, closest to the trees, but Sara wisely didn't take them in a straight line. Doric ambled along beside Bethda, who kept staring at her and tripping over her feet.

"That is really magnificent," she said. "Why were you in our bathroom?"

Doric couldn't answer, so she made a low grumbling sound that she hoped was reassuring. Bethda giggled.

At last they reached the house. Sara motioned them all to come close, even though Doric took up quite a bit of room. She leaned forward conspiratorially.

"Here's what I'm thinking," Sara said. "Stupidface is home, thinking he can carry on however he likes and Bethda won't find out about him. Which is ridiculous. There are only like forty people in this village. But anyway, Isla will scream, because she is the best at it, and he'll come out because he thinks he's a hero. I'll pretend to be fighting our new friend here, but then you just turn on him and scare him shitless."

"Don't kill him," Laress said. "He's regrettably my cousin, and I like my aunt too much to make her sad."

"Just a little piece," Bethda said. "For me."

Doric stood up on her hind legs and bowed. The girls laughed as quietly as they could, which wasn't very.

"All right," said Sara. "Whenever you're ready, Isla."

Isla strolled over closer to the window of the hut, cracked her neck, and let loose the most blood-freezing scream Doric had ever heard. It was very hard to keep from laughing, but somehow everyone managed. Isla followed up with a few cries for help while she was running towards the forest. Doric stamped around in the brush, kicking up a lot of noise.

A young man came charging out of the house, brandishing an axe. When he saw that Sara was, apparently, holding off a giant beast with only her shortsword, he immediately rushed to her rescue. He didn't even notice that anyone else was there. As soon as he was committed, Sara leaned out of the way, kissed Doric's paw, and ran off.

Doric turned towards the boy and rose up on her hind legs. He had immediate second thoughts, and his backpedaling allowed her to reach down and take the axe. She threw it casually over her shoulder and roared, reaching for him with her paws. The boy screamed even louder than Isla had and turned tail to run. Doric fell forward, carefully swiping her talons through his hair and avoiding any actual bloodletting. He ran into the house and slammed the door shut. They could hear the noise of him piling furniture up in front of it.

"That," said Bethda, "was the greatest thing I have ever seen."

"I think he wet himself," Laress said.

Doric reverted back to her usual shape and held out a lock of hair to Bethda.

"Oh, this is perfect!" she said, holding it in both hands. "He's so vain about his hair. He probably won't come outside for a week."

"Thank you," Sara said, running up. "That was much better than anything we could have come up with."

"You're welcome," said Doric. "I have to get back to the tavern, though."

"Come visit anytime!" Bethda said, still swaying on her feet but looking much happier about how the night was going.

The other girls agreed, but they were drunk, and Doric wasn't sure how far she could believe them. At least they hadn't been afraid of her. These strangers, who didn't *have* to like her—not as part of a circle or clan—hadn't cared. It wasn't the perfect test, but it was a start.

She made her way back to the tavern and found Jowenys hadn't moved. She was still happily chatting away with the dwarves, who were now unrolling blue-prints of ship designs. Jowenys smiled when Doric sat down. Yes, it had been a pointless diversion, but Doric felt better than she had in days, and much calmer about going back to the wood elves with her new powers. She decided that was good enough for now.

Doric's first hunting expedition could have gone better.

When she was twelve and Torrieth was fourteen, they had decided that they were more than ready to learn to use a proper bow and arrow. Or, rather, Torrieth had decided, and Doric had not said no. They had been using practice weapons on the archery range where the grown-up rangers practiced, but those arrows were blunted and didn't stick very well. Torrieth wanted her shots to land.

Torrieth's father really should have known better than to leave his weapons lying around. The bow was much too big for the girls to string, but they could use his arrows. Torrieth even put them in her own practice quiver to smuggle them down from the village and into the woods. Doric was much less comfortable with the plan, but once Torrieth got on a roll, it was easier to follow along.

"You're the best, Doric," Torrieth said once they were in the shelter of the trees. "Anyone else would have chickened out by now. You never get scared of anything."

Doric was scared all the time, but the things she was afraid of were too difficult to explain.

"I just don't want to get in trouble," she said. "You can charm your way out of anything, but your uncle always glares at me like it's my fault."

"Mama says Uncle Marlion enjoys blaming other people for his problems," Torrieth said breezily. "I'd never let you take the blame. You know that, right?"

"Of course I do," Doric said. It just didn't always matter.

The girls crept farther into the forest. It was important that they avoid any actual hunting parties, but Torrieth wasn't swayed. Doric hadn't killed her own food since she came to live with the wood elves and wasn't in a particular hurry to get back to it. She understood that, for Torrieth, this was an important part of growing up and being accepted. Doric always understood acceptance.

They got close to a place where Torrieth knew there was a rabbit warren. It was the wrong time of day for a rabbit hunt, but Torrieth was determined. They took up their positions by one of the rabbit holes and waited. Doric could wait forever, but Torrieth's mind usually wandered quickly. Doric expected her to give up after a couple of hours, but the wood elf was unusually focused. The sun reached its peak and started its descent, and still they waited.

"Your father has definitely missed his arrows by now," Doric whispered.

"Then there's no point going back empty-handed," Torrieth said.

Just when Doric was ready to plead for a return, a fat rabbit poked its head out of the warren. Torrieth held her breath and raised an arrow to the string. She waited while the rabbit tested the air, looking for predators, but they had picked their spot well, and the rabbit didn't smell them. After a few more moments, the rabbit came out of the hole entirely.

Torrieth's bowstring twanged as she let the arrow fly, but the shot went wide. Doric couldn't imagine what had gone wrong. Torrieth hadn't shot that badly in years, and surely the arrows didn't make that much of a difference. Then she realized that Torrieth was crying.

"Did you hurt yourself?" Doric asked.

"No," Torrieth snapped. "I just wasn't expecting it to be so cute!"

Her outrage was the last straw. Doric's anxiety over getting caught changed to hysteria, and she started to laugh.

"It's not funny," Torrieth said, but she was already starting to smile.

She went and retrieved the arrow and returned it to her quiver.

"I guess we should go home," she said. "Don't worry. I'll explain everything. Just never tell anyone what happened, or I'll never speak to you again."

Doric knew it wasn't a real threat—none of Torrieth's threats were real—but she never said a word.

CHAPTER 20

Doric was ready to go early in the morning. If Jowenys thought she was excited to get home, Doric let her think that. The truth was that she wanted to get out of the village before she crossed paths with any of the girls from last night. It had been fun, but Doric wasn't quite ready to share it yet. They made for the forest, both of them relaxing as soon as they were under the eaves. It didn't take very long for Doric to hear a familiar bird call. The hunting party arrived shortly after Doric heard the call. Deverel got to the clearing first, but he was smart enough not to get in the way as Torrieth came barreling out of the brush. She threw herself

into Doric's arms, and Doric surprised herself by returning the hug almost as enthusiastically.

"You're home!" crowed Torrieth. "You're home."

She settled down enough to take a few steps back.
In the near year that Doric had been away, Torrieth
hadn't changed very much. The older girl was a bit taller,
but that was the only difference. Doric knew that the
same could not be said of herself. She carried herself
differently now. She took up more space.

"Look at you!" Torrieth said. "Did you grow? Is it
just that you stopped slouching? Green is definitely
your color. Do you have to wear it all the time now?"

"Give the girl some space." Fenjor appeared from
the trees. He hadn't rushed, and Doric noticed he was
limping. That wasn't a good sign. "And where are your
manners, Torrieth? Doric, who is your companion?"

"This is Jowenys," Doric said.

"I'm a druid. And Doric's roommate," Jowenys volunteered. Several of the elves reacted to the second half
of the announcement with clear surprise. "I mean, she
didn't have a choice, but she seems to like me."

Fenjor laughed.

"Welcome, both of you," he said. "Now, let's get back
to the camp before Liavaris sends out a search party for
our search party."

"She knew we were close?" Doric asked.

"The rangers did," Torrieth said. "So she sent us out
to check."

Doric noticed that both Torrieth and Deverel were
wearing ranger colors. She was very proud of them.
Doric had hoped they would be moving up in the ranks

by the time she returned, and she was glad to see that they were.

"I want to hear everything," Torrieth said. "Have you been on a ship? Did you meet anyone scary? Did you get to eat anything amazing?"

Jowenys was more than happy to talk, and Doric let her. As her newest friend chattered away with her oldest, Doric felt herself drift to the side. Even with Torrieth's arm linked through hers, she wasn't really necessary. It was exactly what she expected, and somehow that made it hurt less. Torrieth squeezed her arm as they walked, every time Jowenys answered for both of them. Doric hoped that meant that she understood, but she was too afraid to ask and get the answer for herself.

DORIC WANTED TO scout by herself to keep the elf clan out of any danger, but her decision was overruled by Torrieth almost as soon as she said it. Jowenys, who was much less familiar with the Neverwinter Wood, agreed. Doric felt a bit of a sting over it but didn't press the issue.

"I know you have only just arrived," Fenjor said. "We were on our way to the original camp that you and Torrieth discovered last spring and diverted to meet you. I was hoping you'd be able to come with us. We'd only planned to scout, but with the pair of you, we might become a strike team instead."

"That works for me," Doric said. "Is that camp still the closest to our village?"

"Yes," said Torrieth. "And it's the farthest upriver as well. The humans are staying south and southwest, near their city as much as they can."

"Our concern is that as they run out of sizable trees, they'll push farther into the forest," Fenjor said. "They've also started clear-cutting strips of the forest. It's wasteful. They leave the smaller trees and shrubs to rot, and they don't seem to care."

Doric looked at the map Fenjor had sketched out with the lumber camps added to it. There were so many of them, and it was enraging to see the woods encroached upon. She felt a familiar roar growing in her chest and knew it was only a matter of time until she got to let it out.

"All right," Doric said. "I understand why you want to come with us, but I still think that Jowenys and I should take the lead."

Torrieth started to protest, but Doric cut her off.

"If the humans catch sight of you, what do you think they'll do?" Doric asked. "If we can make them think it's magic as much as possible, the clan will be safer in the long run."

"Doric's right, Torrieth," Fenjor said. "This is why we sent for her, remember?"

Torrieth looked like she wanted to argue, but she held her tongue.

"All right, then," Doric said. She looked up at the sky, to the gray clouds ahead. It was gloomy in the forest, but she didn't need her fur lining anymore. "Ready your weapons, and we'll head out."

The elves peeled away to make last-minute preparations. Torrieth didn't look at any of them. Fenjor sighed and patted Doric on the shoulder.

"She missed you," Fenjor said. "She wants you here, and she wants you to be happy. That makes her a little emotional, and I don't think that's a bad thing."

Doric nodded. She had missed Torrieth, too. Even with Jowenys beside her, nothing could match the sense of unwavering friendship Torrieth had always offered her, even before Doric knew what it was. But Torrieth wasn't the whole clan, and it was critical that Doric prove herself here. This was what she had been training so hard for.

The wood elves returned. It was a small party. Fenjor, Torrieth, and Deverel, six other rangers, and the two druids. Everyone except Jowenys was armed with projectiles and wearing light leather armor. Jowenys had her staff. Fenjor led the way to the lumber camp. Every recognizable rock and tree sent up alarms in Doric's head. The humans were too close. If they pushed back against the elves, it would be dangerous. Doric had the uncomfortable feeling that it was more a matter of when.

Fenjor stopped them about two hundred yards from the clearing. Doric could hear the river, which was a good sign, because that meant the humans hadn't dammed it up yet. It also gave them a bit of cover as they ranged out over the dry brush to take their positions. The elves were under instructions not to fire an arrow unless they had to, but the rangers were ready to cause a distraction or lead the humans on a merry chase if necessary.

Doric and Jowenys crept forward, stooped low with their weapons at the ready. Neither of them made a sound as they went through the brush, even though there were dried pine needles and cracked leaves. They looked out over the lumber camp together, scanning for where the humans were and planning their attack.

It seemed like there were hundreds of them. Chopping wood, removing branches, sawing and hacking at venerable trunks, mindless of the damage to trees that were older than many of them combined. Even more of the humans were on patrol, wandering back and forth across the clearing with their hands on their hilts. They were well armed. Whoever was funding them had the money to do it properly.

The devastation was worse than Doric had been expecting, even after hearing Fenjor describe the clear-cutting. It seemed like there were hacked-off stumps as far as she could see, stretching out like so many truncated futures the forest would never grow. The underbrush was a mess of drag marks as smaller plants and funguses were flattened by uncaring boots and sledges. Even the smell was wrong.

Worst of all was the sound. It wasn't silence; silence would have been better. Forests could be silent, in their own way. But this was nothing like that. Gone was the creak of aged trunks in the wind. The rasp of branches as trees that interlocked in the canopy brushed together. The whisper of the leaves. There was no rustle of small game in the brush, no chatter of squirrels hiding nuts, no hungry cries of new-hatched birds reaching upward for that first mouthful of worm. There was the scrape of metal through wood and the stamp of horse on ground. The laughter of humans and, each blow so distinct that Doric was almost sick, the steady thwack of axes.

"This is only one camp," Jowenys breathed in her ear.

Doric barely heard her over the rage that rose up inside her. They dared! They dared to ruin her forest, her home. They dared to upset the balance of nature so egregiously that the very landscape changed beneath their axes. She was going to destroy them.

Jowenys grabbed her sleeve, bringing Doric back to the moment. Their party was too small for direct confrontation with so many, but Doric and Jowenys knew how to be indirect. They crept back to the elves.

"There's too many of them," Fenjor said. "We should get reinforcements."

"No," Doric said. "Jowenys and I will take care of this group now, and then we can get reinforcements to hit the other camps."

"We're not leaving you!" Torrieth protested.

"Yes, you are," Doric told her. "We'll make them run away, and then we'll break everything. They won't know it's us."

Fenjor didn't look happy, but he was nodding. Torrieth stomped away.

"Don't worry if you hear strange animals," Jowenys said. "It'll just be us."

Doric knew it was about to get stranger than Jowenys was expecting. The two of them gave the elves some time to retreat from the clearing and hammered out a plan quickly. Fenjor made a couple of suggestions before he left to join the others. Jowenys squeezed Doric's hand, and the girls split up so that they could attack from different sides.

Doric watched as Jowenys turned herself invisible and then passed without a trace to a large stack of logs. Doric didn't see Jowenys's next spell, but she felt the roll of it in the ground. The earth shook, radiating out from the epicenter of Jowenys standing near the log pile, and the whole thing collapsed. Doric listened and after a few moments heard the bird call that signified Jowenys was all right and had reached the other side of the clearing.

The guards were not listening for bird calls. As soon as the log pile collapsed, half a dozen of them ran over with swords drawn to investigate. Doric listened to them shout at one another, and then she pulled herself together for her attack.

She hissed an incantation through her teeth and conjured up a spectral wolf, sending it racing towards the humans. They had stopped their work when the commotion began, but when the wolf appeared in front of them, they fled, screaming, towards the water. The wolf didn't chase them too quickly, but it did nip at their heels every now and again, just for fun. More guards went after them, but they couldn't seem to catch the wolf. When they splashed into the water, the wolf turned away and melted back into the forest. Just as they were starting to relax a little bit, the wolf howled. The humans shrieked and finished crossing the river so that they could be closer to the bonfire in the center of the camp.

As a last-minute decision, Doric sent a blast towards the humans who were stripping the logs. It was simple; she didn't shake the earth as much as Jowenys had, but it was still effective. They hadn't even hit anyone yet, and most of the humans looked ready to flee. From the other side of the clearing, Jowenys whistled again. She was going to Wild Shape, leaving the final play up to Doric.

Doric changed into the owlbear as smoothly as she might have slid a tunic over her head. She was massive, bigger than any grizzly, and her talons scraped large tears into the ground as she flexed her paws. This was who she was: power and fury, balance and reckoning, rage and precision. A few of the humans had already seen her and were starting to shout. Doric charged straight at the largest remaining pile of logs, bellowing the owlbear's screech, and tore it apart.

Everyone noticed her at that point.

The unarmed humans broke. Dropping their tools and burdens, they fled towards the city of Neverwinter. A few of the guards followed them, but at least two dozen stood their ground. None had crossbows, but two of them were archers. Doric went after them first. Her long legs and powerful haunches propelled her across the clearing. One of them got a pitiful shot off, but the arrow went wide in their panic. Then Doric was on them.

Since her targets were the bows and not the archers themselves, she had to be delicate. It was like picking snap peas in Kaliope's garden. She carefully plucked at what she wanted and left the rest behind as though it might keep growing. Without their bows, the archers retreated. Well, one did. The other fainted and did not get up.

After shredding the bows like toothpicks in her talons, Doric turned to face the other guards. Only fifteen or so remained, and they had mustered themselves into some sort of formation. They didn't have any polearms, so Doric simply charged them. The formation broke almost immediately as Doric plowed through, though a few of them did manage to pierce her skin with their blades. It wasn't enough to hurt her badly, but now she was *really* angry. She picked up the guards by the straps on their armor, shook them like rag dolls, and then let them fly. She pecked at them with her terrifying beak and scratched them with her talons. And she roared that bone-piercing screech the entire time.

Vaguely, she was aware of Joweny-as-a-panther harrying any stragglers. Once the guards either fled or were on the ground, Doric smashed through their tents and work areas with abandon, laying waste to everything. This was destruction, yes, but it was also balance. Doric had never felt more powerful.

When it was over, the panther and the owlbear stood panting in the middle of the clearing. The panther couldn't ask questions, but Doric knew it was only a matter of time. She resumed her normal shape, and Jowenys did the same.

She gave the signal that all was well and made her way through the trees as silently as she had come, hoping that was true.

"I CAN'T BELIEVE you can Wild Shape into an owlbear. Why didn't you tell me?" Jowenys crowed when they were all safely back at the main elf camp. "Did you see their faces? It was amazing!"

"No," Torrieth said shortly. "We were too far away to see anything."

She sounded angry about it. Doric didn't know what to say to calm her down. That was usually Torrieth's job when Doric was upset, and Doric was busy right now.

"We did hear the shouting, though," Fenjor said lightly. "That was nice. Though I also have questions."

"Druids usually can't turn into monsters," Jowenys said. "Doric has done something new."

"I'm more concerned that you all decided to just attack the logging camps without consulting with the elders first," Marlion said. "It was supposed to be a scouting mission. You should have come back here, no matter how pressed for time you were. If you've started a war, now we're all in the middle of it."

"No one will know it was us, Marlion," Fenjor said. "Doric made sure of it."

Doric forced herself not to shy away. Torrieth wouldn't talk to her, and there were too many questions on Fenjor's face. Marlion looked troubled, uncomfortable with the revelation of what Doric had done. Liavaris said nothing but held Doric's hand as they sat by the fire.

Talking strategy seemed to make Torrieth feel better. She, Jowenys, and the rangers talked about their ideas, ranging from deadfalls to actual animals the rangers could bring in. Marlion reminded them that the goal was mischief, not murder, which limited their options. Fenjor argued that there was no reason the wood elves should keep their hands completely bloodless. The humans were invading, even if it was an unconventional invasion. They were destroying the land. After a few hours, they seemed to have reached an accord. Torrieth still wasn't smiling, but at least she was no longer seething. Doric retired for the night without speaking to her, unwilling to risk the fragile peace.

The following day, more groups went out, each heading for a different lumber camp. They were told to be careful and leave no traces, but Doric couldn't help feeling that this was a mistake, even though agreeing with Marlion felt strange. They had no idea who was behind the lumber operation, no idea what resources they were up against. Doric would have gathered more information before plunging into a fight, but the wood elves were determined to take matters into their own hands. Doric might have argued harder, but it was hard to fight her clan.

The next twenty-four hours saw undeniably good results. The wood elves fought without rest, flitting from camp to camp, wreaking havoc everywhere. The humans withdrew from several camps altogether. Deverel arranged for a small rockfall to take out a carefully stacked log delivery. Jowenys and Doric continued to torment the humans with magic. Doric tried to be as focused as possible, but even she got caught up in the thrill of their success. She didn't change into the owlbear again, though. She and Jowenys agreed that it was too memorable.

The wood elves were pleased with their progress, and Doric was just starting to feel cautiously optimistic when the scouts came back the following morning to give their report. She knew it was nothing they'd hope to hear as soon as she saw their faces.

"The good news is that the humans seem willing to believe that the Neverwinter Wood is haunted," said one scout. "They know there's magic here, and so they've convinced themselves that the woods are against them."

"What's the bad news?" asked Doric. No one looked like that and started with "the good news is" unless the bad news was very bad.

"They're bringing in more guards," the second scout reported. "A *lot* more guards. It's basically an army stationed at a lumber camp now. And the civilian woodcutters are starting to fight back. They're not trained, but they've still got axes. We could fight them off, but only one camp at a time, and we'd have to use a lot more direct force, not just the tactics we've been using."

"Plus, they'll just call in even more reinforcements," the first scout said. "We could risk luring one camp's guards to another camp, I suppose, but then we'd face too many of them at once. We wouldn't be able to spare anyone to attack the vulnerable camp."

"It's definitely too dangerous," Doric agreed. "The only thing keeping you safe from a direct response is the fact that they don't suspect the wood elves."

"Us," said Torrieth, her voice sharp.

"What?" said Doric. She looked up from the map abruptly and found that Torrieth was glaring at her.

"The only thing keeping *us* safe," Torrieth clarified, softening slightly. She was looking at Doric like she barely recognized her anymore, and it hurt more than Doric could have imagined. "This is your home, too."

"Of course," Doric stumbled. She would fight for them as long as she could, but she didn't want them to get hurt in the process. She hadn't been able to save Leander, and it had almost crushed her. If something happened to Torrieth or one of the others while they were fighting something that was too big for them, she'd never forgive herself. "I just meant—"

"It doesn't matter," Torrieth said, all softness disappearing. "What matters is that now we're stuck with even more guards and more logging, and it's like we didn't make any progress at all."

Doric froze. It was every nightmare she'd ever had, every worry that Leander had put into her head, and the fact that it was coming from Torrieth made it a thousand times worse. Doric wanted to run, to fly away as fast as she could.

"I'm sorry," Doric said. It felt like her soul was being pulled up her throat. "I didn't mean to make it worse. You probably should have sent for a different druid."

Then she turned, Wild Shaped into a jackrabbit, and fled into the trees. Torrieth called out after her, voice high and desperate, but Doric didn't slow down.

CHAPTER 21

All Doric wanted was to get out of the woods. Her jackrabbit legs pumped, sending her across the forest floor in a streak of brown fur. The trees thinned, and the air became noticeably colder. Her rabbit lungs didn't care, but now that she was out in the open, a prey animal was probably not the best choice. Doric resumed her own shape, and her tail was restless. She tucked it up under her short cape and started walking.

She found a woodcutters' track before long and followed it along the edge of the woods. The people who actually lived here, who made their living in the forest, weren't her problem. They knew which trees to take and which to leave, and they mostly stuck to the edges. Absently, she wondered how they felt about the logging being done inside the forest. Were they jealous that they weren't getting a cut, or, like the elves, did they view it as an invasion of their home?

Smoke was rising in the distance, gray streams running up from a few chimneys. Doric knew she must be close to some of the villages over here; humans tended to prefer living together rather than in isolated homesteads. She didn't want to run into anyone by accident, so she left the track and headed back into the woods.

She wandered through a section of forest where new saplings had been planted. They wouldn't be large enough to cut for decades, and yet the woodcutters had planned ahead. There were trees left standing while their neighbors were cut, because they had nests or because they were too young, or even because their trunks weren't straight enough. There was balance here, after all. Doric felt herself calming down. Surely there was a balanced answer to her problem, and when she slowed down enough, she would find it.

After the new saplings, Doric started passing older trees. They were in rows, so she knew they had been planted, but the underbrush was the same as in the untouched part of the forest. She crossed back into the old growth and had to pay closer attention to the ground so that she didn't trip over any roots as the light faded.

There were fire marks on the ground. Not a forest fire—they were too small, and the elves would have said something. A group of people had camped here, more than once, like they were scouting for something. Doric felt a lump of dread in her throat at the idea of what they might be scouting for.

She looked up when she detected movement. A piece of red fabric was tied to the branch of a tree, and it was fluttering in the wind. The tree was an oak, which Doric didn't think much of until she found a second oak tree that was similarly marked. After passing five red cloths flapping in the evening breeze, Doric had a horrible suspicion about what the scouts were looking for.

A soft hoot caught her attention, and she saw the owl. She realized that she was much closer to the owl's glade than she had thought.

There was an oak tree in the owl's glade. The glade where she had begun her path as a druid. The glade where Sunmuir had left the armor for her.

Doric transformed into a panther and ran through the trees. She made good time, and with her cat eyes, she could see quite clearly in the gathering dark. She arrived at a new logging camp just after nightfall. It wasn't on the map that Fenjor had used, but it was clearly well established. A large fire was burning, and a few of the humans were passed out around it, but enough were awake to keep her on her guard.

"We shouldn't have trusted Gaspard," one of them was ranting. He swayed back and forth on his feet, and Doric could smell him from where she crouched. "He's gone off after some magic tree and left some of us behind so he doesn't have to share the treasure with all of us."

While the others groused about it, Doric felt her heart skip a beat. There was only one tree in the Neverwinter Wood that she knew of that could be considered magic, and she wore the treasure the tree had been protecting on her forearms. Her suspicions about the owl's tree were confirmed. The logging scouts were very drunk, but she had no way of knowing how long ago the others had left. She had no time to lose.

A soft whickering noise came from upwind. The humans had picketed their horses, and they hadn't smelled Doric's panther-shape yet. She had to be on her way, but she knew it wouldn't take long to spook the horses into bolting. In their state, the humans might never find them, and they'd just wander home to their stables. She circled around so that the horses were downwind of her, and they started to get nervous. They stamped and whinnied as she got closer. By the time they saw her—cat-shaped and yellow-eyed in the night—they were already pulling at their tethers. They broke and fled when she hissed at them, charging right through the camp, which was a nice bonus.

Doric turned her back to the chaos and ran.

THE HUMANS REACHED the glade with the druid's tree just before she did. From a distance, she could see that they had several torches, and one of them was holding something that glimmered in the firelight. She knew it was an axe even before she got close enough to make it out. The human holding it looked unfortunately sober, and Doric knew she had only a little bit of time before the destruction started.

A deep hooting filled the glade. Doric looked up and saw the snowy owl perched in the highest branches of the tree. Its wings were spread wide, like it was about to dive down on the intruders below. They were much bigger than the prey the owl hunted, though, and Doric didn't think it would end well if the owl made the dive. The humans heard the noise and paused, but one of them fired an arrow at the owl, and the man with the axe resumed his advance.

Doric was owlbear-shaped before she knew it. She was furious that these humans and their greed wouldn't leave her alone. Every time she thought she had a moment of peace or a good understanding with her friends, some human like Leander came along and messed it up. Every time she thought she'd found a nice human, like Cassa or Kaliope, she found ten more who were terrible and selfish, like her parents. She could never truly trust them, and that made her angry. With a roaring screech that put the snowy owl's call to shame, she crashed into the glade, ready for a fight.

These humans were made of sterner stuff than the boy Doric had frightened off for Bethda. Two of them dropped their torches, and the lick of flame spread through the grass. Doric was going to have to fight people and fire at the same time, but the people were still the biggest threat.

She swung her taloned paws at the closest person, sweeping him off his feet and into a tree. He stumbled, trying to regain his balance, but his arm was at the wrong angle. Doric moved on to her next target. She screeched in the archer's face and stepped on her bow, shattering it with her weight. The archer crawled off, pulling herself away from the fire and Doric at the same time.

By now, the humans had wised up and decided not to face a fire and an owlbear at the same time. Only the man with the axe remained, and he had used the distraction to bury the axe in the tree. Doric screamed at him, but he swung again. The owl swooped down, flapping at his eyes and scraping at his head with its talons. He flailed about with the axe in confusion, and Doric caught it in her flank. It was a glancing blow, not enough for the axe to embed itself in her side, but she screamed, the owlbear suddenly fighting against her. There was nothing else she could do but resume her own shape. There was a flash of victory in the man's eyes when he saw her, a small girl with a wound, but Doric rolled to her feet with Sunmuir's knives in her hands.

Shrieking insults she hardly understood, Doric threw herself at the man. He was so startled by her ferocity in her own form that he was slow to swing the axe, and she avoided it easily. Once she was inside his guard, it was all over. She cut his arms and chest, slashing too quickly for him to counter. He cried out in pain and dropped the axe. He tried to come back to fight her with his fists, but he was unsteady on his feet and stumbled into the flames. He fled, screaming like a torch, until finally Doric was alone.

When she was absolutely sure everyone was gone, Doric collapsed to her knees, checking her side. The owl was still flying, circling the glade with increasing desperation. Doric had a moment of utter panic, and then she remembered what she was and brought a cascade of water down to extinguish the flames. The interlopers were gone, and the fire was smoldering. Doric was exhausted, but she made a fall of water one more time, to make certain the fire was quenched.

The owl landed back on the tree branch. Doric held one hand up to the axe scar that now marred its trunk. She thought to apologize, but the owl reached a wing down and ghosted it against her face. It wasn't the whole forest. She couldn't save the whole forest by herself. But she had saved this part of it, the part where she had found her direction and learned to face the memories that hurt her so much. She had done enough.

Doric walked back to the wood elf village slowly. The sun was rising, and she had made it only as far as a little stream with a familiar washed-out bank. She couldn't think of any reason not to, so she curled up in the hollow there and let herself sleep.

Liavaris found her there, of course, her knees pulled up and her arms and tail wrapped around them so she could fit into the little washout that had once been her home. The elf elder sat down next to her, knees creaking, and leaned her head back against the hill.

"You know, for someone who had no idea what they were doing, the place you picked to camp when you got here is pretty nice," she said. "Gets a good bit of morning sun."

"I just picked it because I'd have to build only one wall," Doric croaked.

"Also clever," Liavaris said.

"I ruined everything," Doric told her. "All you wanted was for me to become a druid so that I could help, and I've only made it worse."

"Oh, Doric," Liavaris said. She wrapped an arm around Doric's shoulders. "All I wanted was for you to be trained by the best people so that you could be the best. I knew that would make you happy. It wasn't a bargain with fine print. I didn't feed you all these years because I was hoping to get a fancy guard dog out of it. I love you."

Doric choked.

"You what?" she asked.

"Ever since I found you, you've been strange and wonderful," Liavaris said. "I didn't have my own children, but I did have you, and I wouldn't trade you for anything. I should have told you all the time. You were so prickly when you were little. I thought you'd run away if I smothered you, so I held my tongue. That was a mistake. I'm sorry that I ever made you feel unwelcome or unwanted."

"I thought—" Doric stumbled.

"No one is universally liked, even in their own clan," Liavaris said. "I can't stand Marlion, and he knows it. That's probably at least part of why he was always such a jerk to you. But all I wanted was for you to know that you had a home, whenever you wanted it, and I'm sorry if I ever made you feel otherwise."

Doric leaned against her, finally quiet.

"Torrieth hates me," she said.

"Torrieth misses you," Liavaris said. "And she's scared. And she's intimidated by Jowenys because, for the longest time, you needed her for everything, and now you don't. But she'll work it out. She just needs a bit of time."

Doric watched the water rushing by. It didn't look like there had been another flood since the one that brought her and Liavaris together. Fate was funny like that.

"They really don't blame me?" Doric asked.

"They know you did what you could," Liavaris said. "Some things are just too big, even for you."

Doric wanted to sit on this stream bank for the rest of her life while she digested everything Liavaris had just told her. It was like the owlbear. As soon as Liavaris had said it, she knew that it was true. There was a fundamental shift inside her, and now everything was different.

"I'm ready to go back now," Doric said.

"I'll always be waiting for you," Liavaris said.

And the little girl in the attic, the one with the window and the dream, and the parents who had left her alone in the forest, knew that it was true.

Doric smiled.

LIAVARIS WATCHED AS HER SELF-APPOINTED ward healed from her ordeal in the forest and wished that there were more that she could do. Doric's body was mending fine, but Liavaris worried about her spirit and her mind. She had been enraged when Doric had calmly told her about being abandoned by her parents. It had taken all of her control to keep her voice even. She'd paid Doric a compliment to make the girl feel better. She hadn't wanted her anger to seep through and scare her.

Doric scared easily. It wasn't the usual sort of fears that children had. She didn't fear the dark, because she could see in it, and she wasn't afraid of monsters, because she had already survived them. She feared the river. She feared the quiet. And she feared being left alone.

Torrieth was a blessing when it came to the latter. The elfling had all but staked a claim on Doric's friendship, and the harder her uncle disapproved, the harder Torrieth hung on. It wasn't just stubbornness or pity, even if that was how it started. Liavaris could see the genuine affection that Torrieth had for Doric, and it made her feel more secure as Doric's guardian.

She knew Doric kept packs of food and other supplies stashed around the camp. She didn't even steal things for them, merely saved from what she was given. She was unusually good at not being a burden, which made Liavaris's heart ache. No child should have that skill. Liavaris wouldn't dream of taking the packs away, and she hoped she never did anything that made Doric think she would need them. Marlion might carry on, and a few of the others might agree with him, but Liavaris had decided that Doric was hers, and that meant she was staying. They would just have to get used to it.

Slowly but steadily, Liavaris coaxed Doric out of her shell. They learned her favorite foods together, and what colors she liked when it came to clothing. Doric eventually let her brush and cut her hair. The first time they tried, she was wound so tight Liavaris thought she might bolt. She talked more. She laughed. She voiced the occasional opinion.

She never strayed far from Liavaris or Torrieth. A few of the other wood elves, particularly those with young children, tried to extend kindness to her, but Doric curled up like a fern when they tried. Liavaris explained to them that it might be a while before Doric could trust adults, and they did their best to understand, but she knew they felt slighted.

She knew because that was how she felt sometimes. She had brought this child into her house and been shown nothing but gratefulness and obedience. It was unnatural. Sometimes Liavaris wondered if it would kill the girl to break something, and then immediately regretted it, because it probably would. She guarded her heart when Doric was around, because she was never sure what would happen if the girl felt the full force of it.

Time passed, and they both grew older. They developed habits and told themselves that it was better this way. Liavaris promised herself that she would love her sweet, feral child and always keep a place for her, even if she could never tell her in so many words. Whatever Doric would accept, she would gladly give.

It wasn't until after Liavaris had sent Doric out into the world that she realized she had never told her that she was loved.

CHAPTER 22

When Doric ran away, Jowenys had decided to send a message to the Enclave and ask for more help. She spoke to Kaliope through an ash tree that Liavaris had babied for a decade. Open was going to teleport over as soon as he could, and since he could go directly from plant to plant, he would be able to get much closer to the camp. While Doric had been away, the elves had not been idle. They knew they couldn't face the human interlopers head-on, so instead they prepared. When Doric returned to the camp, she saw large stacks of arrows, and their blacksmith's little forge was going full tilt to make sure their blades were properly prepared.

"Doric!" Torrieth called out as soon as Doric followed Liavaris into the clearing.

She dropped her fletching and ran across the grass, sweeping Doric up into a hug when she was in reach.

"I'm so glad you're safe," Torrieth said. "Where in the world did you go? I was afraid you'd go back to the Enclave and we'd never see you again."

Usually Doric would shrug off the hug, but this time she let Torrieth's arm rest on her shoulders.

"I went to the owl's glade," Doric said. "Some of the humans had decided to target the oak for magic and treasure."

"Had?" Torrieth asked.

"I took care of it," Doric told her.

"I can't believe you can do that all on your own," Torrieth said. "I mean, I've seen it, but it's still amazing. How many of them did you have to fight?"

"I do have some advantages," Doric reminded her. "I scared off all the horses for the first group, and the second group . . . Well, it might be easier to show you without any obstacles or distractions. You didn't get to see it either of the times I fought like this, and you should have been one of the first people I told."

Doric made her way to the center of the encampment. The main hearth was down to embers because it was midday, and a few elders sat around it. They all greeted Doric, seemingly pleased that she had returned. Doric made sure there was enough space and then motioned for everyone to step away from her.

"Remember, it'll still be me," she told them as she

started climbing down the ladder with Torrieth right behind her. "I'll just be, uh, bigger."

First she turned into the panther, making a show of flicking her tail at Torrieth's head. Doric did one loop of the biggest tree in the camp in the panther shape and then gathered herself to shift again.

As a red-tailed hawk, she streaked up into the sky, her piercing cry echoing through the trees. She circled and dove, let them see her wings and her speed and agility. Torrieth was clapping her hands, and Liavaris looked so proud of her. Even Marlion was impressed.

Doric flapped her wings two more times and prepared for the final Wild Shape. She turned into the owlbear a few feet off the ground, so she landed heavily on all four paws. Then she reared up on her hindquarters and gave a screech-roar she had heard so many times. The wood elves were awestruck. Doric was gigantic and covered in fur and feathers, but it was undeniably still her. Torrieth took a few slow steps forward, reaching out with one hand. Doric lowered herself and tipped her head towards her friend. The fingers that sank into the thick fur of her shoulder didn't hesitate.

"Wow," Torrieth breathed.

Doric turned back into her usual form and bowed.

"That is the most amazing thing I've ever seen!" Deverel declared.

Doric could have made a joke but decided she was done underselling herself. She was powerful, and she could be terrifying. Liavaris loved her anyway, and she wasn't going to hide who she was anymore. Jowenys was clapping, too, and Doric prepared herself for the inevitable interrogation.

"It's pretty fun," Doric told Deverel.

Torrieth took her hand and led her around the wood elf camp. Doric saw all of the fortifications they had made on the ground and in the trees, and Torrieth chattered about things that had changed since Doric left for the Emerald Enclave. None of them were particularly important—new huts and better locations for hearths—but Doric listened to every detail.

"And this is where Deverel and I are going to live," Torrieth said when they reached a new bungalow. The wood planks of the terrace had even been scrubbed.

"Are you getting married?" Doric asked.

"Not for a while," Torrieth said. "But we're sorting out the last few details of the betrothal. I was hoping it would be finished while you were here, actually. I'd like you to be there for the betrothal party. We both would."

"I don't know how much time I'll be able to spend here in the future," Doric told her. "But this will always be home. Unless you move the encampment. Then that will be home."

"I'd send you directions," Torrieth said, grinning.

They sat for a few moments in silence while the camp bustled around them. No one interrupted, even though Doric was getting plenty of inquisitive looks. The children were visibly restraining themselves from pestering her with questions. She appreciated that, but she would make sure to answer some of them later.

"I realize the things I said, about it being 'us,' not 'you,' made it sound like I was angry," Torrieth said after a while. "I was scared and frustrated, so it came out wrong, but I meant it. We need you. I need you. And not because you're a druid. Because you're you."

"It was hard, after my parents abandoned me." Doric had never said the words out loud before. "I was confused more than anything. There were so many things I didn't understand. I was terrified the elders would make me leave or make me stay in the hut. I had to stay in the attic until I was left here, you know. I didn't want my world to be that small again."

Torrieth leaned her head against Doric's shoulder.

"It was easier to think that if I made myself useful, I'd be able to stay," Doric continued. "I wanted to stay so badly. Because I liked you, and I still do."

"Well, that's good," Torrieth said. "Because you're stuck with me." She pointed to the wooden framework of a little home that Doric hadn't noticed, right next to Torrieth's. "That one's for you. For when you need it."

"And for if Deverel gets tired of you snoring." Doric couldn't resist.

"I do not!" Torrieth protested. "You are the worst."

Once upon a time, Doric would have taken that literally. Now, she only laughed.

THEY SETTLED INTO a routine, waiting for Open to appear. Every morning, Doric would sleep in, no longer waking early to help with breakfast. After they all ate, Doric and Torrieth would go out into the forest. They collected berries and acorns, or sometimes looked for sticks that could be used as arrow shafts. It was work, but it was also fun, and Doric relished the combination of the two. Sometimes Deverel or Jowenys came with them, and sometimes not.

In the afternoons, she and the rangers would practice combat and survival tactics. There was some overlap in theory, and Jowenys appreciated learning their techniques. The rangers experimented, too, and soon even the younger ones like Torrieth and Deverel were confident spellcasters.

In the evenings, Doric would sit with Liavaris. Her guardian—her mother, really—had a lot of things she had been holding back from saying over the years, and now Doric was ready to hear them all. Some were stories that were shared around the campfire, but more frequently, the two of them sat apart while Liavaris reminisced about Doric's childhood, and Doric learned to see those memories in a new light.

When the others went to bed, Doric and Jowenys would Wild Shape and go out on patrol. Sometimes Doric ghosted through the remaining lumber camps on soft white wings, looking for weak spots to exploit. The humans were cautious now and had scaled back their operation, but it wasn't over yet. Sometimes Jowenys stalked horses on cat's paws, interrupting supply wagons and forcing the humans to walk everywhere because their mounts had bolted in the night. Occasionally they went down to the woodcutters' village to see what Sara and the other girls were doing. The villagers had begun reaching out to other towns, and

Doric learned that none of them was tied to the destructive logging. The mystery deepened, and she was no closer to solving it.

Despite all of the worries that hung over her head, Doric thrived. She visited the owl's tree after a few days to make sure the bark was healing without infection. She also practiced her healing on any elf or human who needed her. She enjoyed the work, though it left her tired in a different way than her other magic did. Her main strength would always be combat, but there was no harm in practicing other skills. She even got pretty good at it, provided their injuries weren't too serious.

Nothing this idyllic could last forever, and Doric fully expected a plague of locusts or Leander's ghost to appear out of the forest at any moment. Outside the Neverwinter Wood, the seasons marched on. The ground was drier every time Doric patrolled the forest edge. Rumors came from the city of Neverwinter that a new ruler had taken over, but that was far away for now, and Doric had other problems to deal with.

Torrieth and Deverel were betrothed at the end of a hot day, just as the moon was rising. The elves didn't really have finery, but they all had clean clothes for the event, and a few heirloom broaches or pins made an appearance. Torrieth wore a crown of roses, carefully stripped of their thorns. Doric had daisies in her hair. She felt ridiculous, but Liavaris assured her it was lovely. There had been some talk of Doric performing the ceremony, since she was important now, but Doric had immediately refused. Instead, Marlion did it, and he spent the entire time grinning at his niece so widely, Doric thought his face might split.

The dancing lasted for a long time, and instead of sitting to the side, Doric joined in. She skipped and spun, the steps familiar as she lost herself to the music. Jowenys joined in, too, picking up the variations quickly and teaching her own. Eventually Doric was surrounded by elflings who immediately made up a new dance based on her tail. She moved it to the beat while they leapt over it or ducked under it. She tired well before they did, and they were all disappointed when she excused herself, but then Torrieth appeared with a selection of sweets, and that soothed everyone's feelings.

Stuffed full of food and feet sore from dancing, Doric hauled herself into her hut. She thought about going on patrol but decided against it. She deserved a night off, and even though it had been Torrieth and Deverel's betrothal, she still felt like the celebration was in part for her. She wanted to fall asleep in the glow of inclusion while the fires burned down. She could face the real world again tomorrow.

THE REAL WORLD showed up at the crack of dawn when a pair of goshawks dropped out of the sky and landed in the center of the encampment. Doric, who hadn't had any intention of being up this early, dragged herself out of her hut when she heard the commotion of the birds' arrival. She sighed. Her holiday, such as it was, was over.

"Good morning," she said, a little grumpy.

"Good morning!" A cheerful Open appeared where one of the hawks had been. The wood elves were clearly not expecting another tiefling, and they definitely weren't expecting Palanus, but they managed to keep their reactions minimal. "We had to do the last bit the old-fashioned way, but I made excellent time."

"Apparently," Doric said. "I guess now it's my turn to cook *you* breakfast."

CHAPTER 23

Open and Liavaris sized each other up across the hearth. The elder hadn't stayed up too late the night before, so she was reasonably bright-eyed. No one was ever fully prepared to meet Open, though. There was something incongruous about him and the level of attention he gave cooking with cinnamon. The elves who had received a bowl with the extra garnish from him were pretty pleased about it, at least.

"Liavaris, this is Open," Doric said. "He was one of our teachers and also kept us fed. Open, this is my guar—my mother."

Liavaris beamed and shook Open's hand with more

enthusiasm than either of them was expecting. Fine-ground cinnamon arced through the air, and several people sneezed.

"It's wonderful to meet you," Liavaris said. "Besides all the obvious reasons, we're very glad of your help."

"And this is Palanus, another mentor," Doric said. The half-orc bowed their head. "They knew Sunmuir, and I thought maybe they could tell you more about her."

Palanus nodded, and they and Liavaris immediately fell into conversation about druids, both past and present.

"I also have something to show you," Doric said, leaning towards Open. "But it'll have to wait until after breakfast."

They ate quickly, no one saying a word when Open crunched his way through the wooden bowl that held his porridge. He didn't eat the spoon, at least. Doric finished her own breakfast less dramatically, and when she went to wash up, one of Liavaris's nieces took her bowl.

"Go and do druid things, my dear," she said.

Doric led Open and Jowenys into the forest. They told him about the destructive logging and the guards. Doric told almost the whole story of meeting Sara and her friends, though she left out a few of the details in Bethda's revenge plot. Mostly she focused on the work that the woodcutters were doing on the edge of the Neverwinter Wood, and how much more balanced it was than she had expected.

"I think I'll drop in before I go home," Open said.

"I've talked with regular farmers before, but never tree farmers that weren't druids. Maybe they've learned something we have overlooked. Palanus will want to see them as well."

Doric thought that might be a little optimistic, but she didn't think it was a bad idea. If nothing else, Sara would get a kick out of meeting the pair of them.

They entered the little glade, and all three of them quieted, recognizing the sanctity of the place. There were burn marks on the ground, and a few of the trees around the edge of the glade were blackened, but the leaves had grown back, and even the ground shrubs along the scorched fringe of the glade were starting to put out flowers and greenery again. The big tree stood tall, the axe scar almost completely grown over by new bark. There would be no infection via the wound. Doric had made sure of it, even though she couldn't heal the scar itself.

Open laid his hands upon the trunk with some reverence. Doric knew that he probably had the power to heal the scar but didn't think he would. From what she could tell, the tree had already accepted it, and since it wasn't a danger, the tree didn't need it fixed. Open let his hands fall, nodding.

"It's a beautiful place," Open said.

"When I was little, an owl spirit found me," Doric said. "It watched me while I learned how to survive in the forest after my parents abandoned me. I kind of forgot about it. I wanted to forget my parents and all the hurt and fear from my childhood, so I blotted the whole thing out."

"It happens," Open said. "The mind reacts in strange ways to protect itself."

"I lived with Liavaris and hunted with the elf rangers," Doric continued. "They wanted me to join them, but I could never master the necessary tasks. Then I saved Torrieth from a bear by talking to it, and Liavaris remembered what happened when I was young and brought me here. The last druid that lived here, Sunmuir, had left her gear. That's where I got these."

Doric ran her hands down her vambraces, the soft leather still strong and supple.

"I've seen the owl since I came back, too," Doric said. She took a deep breath. Open and Jowenys knew what came next, but she hadn't said the whole thing out loud yet. "There's something I did during the wildfire that I didn't explain to you. I know we were short on time, but I should have made it a priority. I was afraid what you would think of me, but I know better now."

She took several steps away from them, her hands up to indicate that they shouldn't follow. Then she reached for the familiar shape, and her owlbear form filled the glade. Tall and bright white, with sharp beak and talons and thick fur—she was a marvel, not a monster.

"Merciful gods," Open breathed.

"It never stops feeling like that," Jowenys said.

Doric slid back to her own form and smiled crookedly at them.

"The first time, I just did it without thinking," Doric said. "The second time, when I was in the woodcutters' village, was harder, but I was able to think my way through it. Now it's as easy as anything else."

"How do you do it?" Open said. "I've been thinking about it since you left, and I realized that I got so caught up in it that we didn't part very well. I'm sorry that I didn't make it clear that this skill was a good thing."

"Thank you," said Doric. "When I was helping the owlbear, something occurred to me. It had killed Leander, but it wasn't really a monster. It had been driven far south of its normal range, and all it wanted was a den where it could be safe. It picked a place that was too close to a village, and that was the problem. Once I got it out in the wild, everything was fine."

"Except for the gigantic owlbear!" Jowenys said.

"It's hard to explain," Doric said. "I just knew that it wasn't a monster. And I don't think it'll work if I just tell you. It's something you have to know."

"It's incredible, Doric," Open said. "I'm so proud of you."

Doric smiled.

OPEN HAD ACQUIRED a message for Doric at one of the villages he'd passed through on his way. He gave it to her when they returned to the camp.

"I don't know what it is," he said. "Some weird kid just handed it to me and said it was for you, and that you would know who it was from."

"I have no idea who it's from," Doric said. She turned the wrapped parchment over in her hand. There were no identifying marks, just a bit of wax to hold it together.

"Well, he didn't say it was urgent," Open told her.

Doric tossed the letter into her new bungalow as they walked past it. She had moved her things over yesterday, before the betrothal shenanigans began. It got better shade than her previous place did. When she was home, her home would be pleasant.

The others were sitting near the central hearth, discussing what to do next about the logging. Even with help from the woodcutters, the wood elves couldn't fight off all the interlopers alone. The wood elves also had the most to lose, so they had to be extra cautious in their plans.

"We're still targeted," Marlion said. "I don't want to send our hunters and rangers out to fight something they can't match. Doric got their attention, and we need her to deal with it."

"I don't think we're as helpful when it comes to actual fighting," Open said. "Your rangers are better suited than we are."

"Then why did you come all the way here?" Marlion asked. "We have a mess on our hands."

"I came because Doric needed me," Open rumbled. "I'm not going to do nothing. Palanus and I will take Jowenys and work our way south, towards Neverwinter itself. We'll ask the people we see what they've heard and send you messages if we learn anything important."

"And I'll stay," Doric said. "The problem is bigger than our part of the forest. If you hide away, that's fine. I can be the emissary between you and the outside world. If we solve the issue out there, it'll protect you here."

"That seems perfectly reasonable," Liavaris said, cutting off any protestations Marlion might have made.

"We have other business in Neverwinter, something the Emerald Enclave is looking into," Palanus added. "But you don't have to worry about that. You have more than enough to do here."

"Agreed," Liavaris said. "Doric? Do you have anything else to add?"

"No," Doric said. Then a thought occurred to her. "I need a couple of days. There's somewhere I have to go. Alone."

Jowenys started to protest, but Open put his hand on her arm. Torrieth wasn't there, and no one was going to bother her that morning, so Doric didn't get a fight from her either.

"If that's what you have to do," Liavaris said. She looked curious but didn't ask.

"It is," Doric said. "Thank you."

THE DAY AFTER the other druids left for Neverwinter, Doric set out. She wasn't entirely sure where she was going. She hadn't tried to remember the way in a long time. She started at her stream in the morning with the sun behind her and walked.

She was strong now. She could walk for days if she had to. Her tail didn't bother her, and she had taken care of her horns so that they wouldn't itch in the sun. She didn't know how long it would take, because now her legs could take long strides and she didn't have to stop every now and then to frantically fill her stomach with tree bark. All the same, she wasn't really in a hurry. She took her time, enjoying the new spring flowers outside the forest and the warm breezes that carried the smell of green in the air.

She could have traveled as a wolf or a hawk. It would have been faster. But Doric wanted to do this on her own two feet. She found a road but didn't take it. There would be farmers out, tending to their fields and letting their livestock range across the open countryside, and she didn't want to see any of them. Instead, she pressed on through the scrubby hills, the sun starting to heat up the back of her neck.

It was late afternoon when she reached the place where she was going. She knew it by the air and by the feel of the ground beneath her feet. When she looked around, she saw that things were different. It had been years, and many things had changed. But Doric knew where she was, and what it meant that she could stand here. For a moment, she wondered if she ought to speak to them, but then she decided that just being here was enough. They didn't deserve to know what she was now, what they had thrown away because she was inconvenient. Maybe they had already heard legends of her. There was a song circulating taverns about an owlbear who fought bandits. Maybe they sang it and never knew that they could have been part of something great, if they had only cared.

The house was smaller than she remembered, but just as brown. Out front there was a massive vegetable garden, plants growing tall in the season's warmth. The yard was neat, with all the tools carefully stored in the lean-to at the side of the house. There were two animal pens, one with a cow and new calf, the other with a small flock of sheep. The smell of fresh-cut grass was everywhere. There was smoke coming up from the chimney.

Doric expected it to hurt, but it didn't. It was just a house. Even when she looked up and saw the little attic window, she didn't feel anything besides a general rumbling in her belly that reminded her it had been a long time since lunch. This house had taught her to hide, had taught her to fear, but she didn't do that anymore. She went out into the world with her head uncovered and her tail swinging behind her and power at her fingertips. People respected her because of the Emerald Enclave, and people loved her because she was herself. Doric had grown up, and no memory from inside the house had the power to hurt her anymore. She turned away from it, ready to head back home.

And then, because she wasn't perfect, she walked over to the sheep pen, opened the gate, and Wild Shaped into an owlbear.

ACKNOWLEDGMENTS

This was a wild ride.

Thank you to Elizabeth Schaefer, who said no to one thing, and then asked if I wanted to do this instead, and then helped me find my feet. Several times.

Thank you to Josh, as always, for setting things up and humoring me when I send bizarre emoji texts from airports. I'm so glad we're back in airports.

Thank you to Jason Shamblin and Bria LaVorgna, who answered approximately ten million questions with no context and then didn't ask any follow-ups because it's not their first rodeo; and to beccatoria, whom I love, and who wrote a long Twitter thread right after the trailer came out about how owlbears are just *the silliest* and showed me what to avoid.

Thank you to Alice Duke for the outstanding cover, and to the rest of the team at Random House Worlds: Scott Biel, Ella Laytham, Lydia Estrada, Lauren Ealy, Ashleigh Heaton, Pam Alders, Jocelyn Kiker, and Erich Schoeneweiss.

Thank you to Isla for being adorable, even though she gave me a horrifying cold right when I was trying to do revisions. I'm not mad that I named a character after her.

I have not (yet???) met Sophia Lillis, but it was a blast to write her character. I hope she had as much fun as I did.

And thank you to the fans. I kind of forgot that it had been finding out that Chris Pine was playing a bard that had made me sign on to this project, and watching the whole internet go through the emotional journey of finding out together at San Diego Comic-Con was an absolute delight. Special shout-out to saraofswords, who is absolutely correct about drunk girls in a tavern making a great adventuring party.

The Druid's Call was outlined in a cold cottage by a pond, written in a cozy cabin by the sea, and edited in every province in Canada.

ABOUT THE AUTHOR

E. K. JOHNSTON is the #1 *New York Times* bestselling author of several YA novels, including *Star Wars: Ahsoka* and the *Los Angeles Times* Book Prize finalist *The Story of Owen*, which *The New York Times* called "a clever first step in the career of a novelist who, like her troubadour heroine, has many more songs to sing." Her novel *A Thousand Nights* was shortlisted for the Governor General's Award. In its review of *Exit, Pursued by a Bear*, *The Globe and Mail* called Johnston "the Meryl Streep of YA," with "limitless range." Johnston lives in Ontario, Canada.

Twitter: @ek_johnston

ABOUT THE TYPE

This book was set in Caslon, a typeface designed in 1722 by William Caslon (1692–1766). Its widespread use by most English printers in the early eighteenth century soon supplanted the Dutch typefaces that had formerly prevailed. The roman is considered a "work-horse" typeface due to its pleasant, open appearance, while the italic is exceedingly decorative.

A Note from a Sorcerer, Besotted

Dear Doric,

I am sure you will remember me and understand why it is necessary that I write to you. When we last met, I mentioned that I had been through some hard times. I am about to go through some more, and I wanted to ask for your help.

I have heard the most amazing stories about you. The song says that you can turn into an owlbear, which I thought was an exaggeration until a girl with a sword threatened me for questioning it. I suppose if anyone could do it, it would be you.

There's going to be a job. A while ago, some people tried to steal something, and we sort of failed. Well, we stole it, but a couple of them went to prison, and I've been on the run. We're going to set it right, and we need powerful help to do it. As soon as I heard the word "powerful," I thought of you.

I know you're around the Neverwinter Wood. We are also in the area. If we cross paths, I can give you more details, and then you can decide what you are going to do. But I would really like it if you came with ~~me~~ us.

I won't take up too much of your time. I know you are busy doing amazing things.

Yours,
Simon the Sorcerer